Look what people are saying about Jill Shalvis...

"Riveting suspense laced with humor and heart is her hallmark and Jill Shalvis always delivers."
—*USA TODAY* bestselling author Donna Kauffman

"Shalvis firmly establishes herself as a writer of fast-paced, edgy but realistic romantic suspense, with believable and likable supporting characters and fiercely evocative descriptive passages."
—*Booklist*

"For those of you who haven't read Jill Shalvis, you are really missing out."
—*In the Library Reviews*

"Danger, adrenaline and firefighting heat up the mix in Jill Shalvis' blistering new novel."
—*Romantic Times BOOKreviews* on *White Heat*

"Jill Shalvis displays the soul of a poet with her deft pen, creating a powerful atmosphere."
—*WordWeaving*

"Jill Shalvis is a breath of fresh air on a hot, humid night."
—*thereader*

D0616293

Blaze™

Dear Reader,

Over the past few years I've received a bunch of letters asking me to write more firefighter heroes. I responded to those letters with a "hopefully someday." Well, I have good news—someday has come!

In the months ahead I hope you enjoy reading about the sexy firefighters of Firehouse #34, stationed in the fictional beach town of Santa Rey, California. First up is *Flashpoint*. In this book, sexy firefighter Zach Thomas is resisting his attraction to a coworker, all while dealing with the growing suspicion that there is an arsonist in their midst. Then, next month, check out *Flashback,* in which Zach's partner, Aidan Donnelly, solves the mystery and manages to fall hard for a sexy blast from his past. And finally, as a special holiday treat, you'll find one more of these incredible heroes in my contribution to the 2008 Harlequin Blaze Christmas anthology, *Heating Up the Holidays.*

I want to send a great big thanks to all the readers who come to my daily blog. Stop by any time and join me and my friends. I'm looking forward to hearing from you.

Happy reading!

Jill Shalvis
www.jillshalvis.com/blog

JILL SHALVIS
Flashpoint

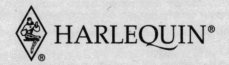

HARLEQUIN®

TORONTO • NEW YORK • LONDON
AMSTERDAM • PARIS • SYDNEY • HAMBURG
STOCKHOLM • ATHENS • TOKYO • MILAN • MADRID
PRAGUE • WARSAW • BUDAPEST • AUCKLAND

If you purchased this book without a cover you should be aware that this book is stolen property. It was reported as "unsold and destroyed" to the publisher, and neither the author nor the publisher has received any payment for this "stripped book."

ISBN-13: 978-0-373-79414-0
ISBN-10:   0-373-79414-2

FLASHPOINT

Copyright © 2008 by Jill Shalvis.

All rights reserved. Except for use in any review, the reproduction or utilization of this work in whole or in part in any form by any electronic, mechanical or other means, now known or hereafter invented, including xerography, photocopying and recording, or in any information storage or retrieval system, is forbidden without the written permission of the publisher, Harlequin Enterprises Limited, 225 Duncan Mill Road, Don Mills, Ontario M3B 3K9, Canada.

This is a work of fiction. Names, characters, places and incidents are either the product of the author's imagination or are used fictitiously, and any resemblance to actual persons, living or dead, business establishments, events or locales is entirely coincidental.

This edition published by arrangement with Harlequin Books S.A.

® and TM are trademarks of the publisher. Trademarks indicated with ® are registered in the United States Patent and Trademark Office, the Canadian Trade Marks Office and in other countries.

www.eHarlequin.com

Printed in U.S.A.

ABOUT THE AUTHOR

USA TODAY bestselling author Jill Shalvis is happily writing her next book from her neck of the Sierras. You can find her romances wherever books are sold, or visit her on the Web at www.jillshalvis.com/blog.

Books by Jill Shalvis

HARLEQUIN BLAZE

 63—NAUGHTY BUT NICE
132—BARED
232—ROOM SERVICE
270—JUST TRY ME...
303—JINXED!
       "Together Again?"
329—SHADOW HAWK

HARLEQUIN TEMPTATION

 938—LUKE
 962—BACK IN THE BEDROOM
 995—SEDUCE ME
1015—FREE FALL

Don't miss any of our special offers. Write to us at the following address for information on our newest releases.

Harlequin Reader Service
U.S.: 3010 Walden Ave., P.O. Box 1325, Buffalo, NY 14269
Canadian: P.O. Box 609, Fort Erie, Ont. L2A 5X3

To the readers of my daily blog.
Having you there with me on my *I Love Lucy*
adventures makes my day, every day.
This firefighter's for you.

Prologue

"Now's your shot with me, Zach. I say we get naked."

Exhausted, filthy, Zach Thomas still managed to lift his head and stare at Cristina. "What?"

Just as filthy, she arched a come-hither brow streaked with soot, which made it difficult to take her seriously. So did the mustache of grime. "You and me," she said. "Naked. What do you think?"

He couldn't help it; he laughed. He thought that she was crazy. They both wore their fire gear and were dragging their asses after several hours of intense fire-fighting. All around them, the stench of smoke and devastation still swirled in thick gray clouds, penetrating their outfits, their skin. Nothing about it felt sexy.

"Hey, nobody laughs at my offer of sex and lives," she told him. "Not even you, Officer Hottie."

When he grimaced at the nickname, she laughed. "You doing me tonight or not?"

Sex as a relaxant worked—generally speaking, sex as anything worked—but Zach was so close to comatose he couldn't have summoned the energy to pull her close, much less do anything about it once he got her that way. "I can't."

"Now we both know that's a lie."

Firefighting left some people exhilarated and pumped

with adrenaline. Cristina was one of them. Normally he was, too, but they'd just lost a civilian—an innocent young kid—and he couldn't get that out of his head. "I can't," he repeated.

Cristina sighed. She was in her midtwenties, blond, and so pretty she could have passed for an actress playing a firefighter, but she was the real deal, as good as any guy on the squad. She was also tough-skinned, cynical and possessed a tongue that could lash a person dead without trying.

He should know; he'd been on the wrong end of it plenty of times. So he braced himself, but she just sighed again. As sardonic and caustic as she could be, they really were friends. Twice they'd been friends with benefits, but it had been a while. She let it go, rolling her eyes at him, but moving off, leaving him alone.

He stood there a moment more, surrounded by chaos, his gear weighing seventy-five pounds but feeling like three hundred as the radio on his hip squawked. Allan Stone, their new chief, was ordering everyone off the scene except the mop-up crew, who would stay through what was left of the night to make sure there were no flare-ups. Tommy Ramirez, the fire inspector, was already on scene, his job just beginning.

Zach's crew was slowly making their way to their respective rigs. He needed to move, as well, but his gut was screaming on this one—someone had set this blaze intentionally. Unfortunately, it wasn't the first time he'd suspected arson when no one else had. Even more unfortunately, the last two times he'd thought so, he'd been reprimanded by Tommy for having an "authority" issue.

He didn't.

Okay, maybe he had a *slight* authority issue, sometimes, but not tonight.

He could ask Aidan what he thought but Zach knew what his firefighting partn and best friend would say. *Grab a beer, a woman and a bed, in any order.* And if Zach called Cristina back, he could knock out two of the three. Yeah, that was what he should do.

So why he headed toward the burned-out shell of a house instead, he had no idea, except that he trusted himself enough to know something was off here.

Something big.

And he couldn't just walk away from it.

He never could.

1

BROOKE WAS A VIRGIN. Not in the classic sense of the word—that status had changed on her seventeenth Halloween night when she'd dressed as an evil, slutty witch and given in to a very naughty knight in shining armor— but that was another story.

She was a *California* virgin, but as she drove up the coast for the first time and into the small town of Santa Rey, she lost that cherry, as well.

Santa Rey was a classic West Coast beach town, mixing the best elements of Mexico and Mediterranean architecture, all within steps of the beach shimmering brilliantly on her left. There were outdoor cafés, shops and art galleries, skateboarders and old ladies vying for the sidewalks with surfers and snotty tourists, and if she hadn't been so nervous, she might have taken the time to enjoy it all more.

She took a last glance at her quickly scrawled directions, following them to Firehouse 34. Parking, she peered through her windshield at the place, nerves wriggling like pole dancers in her belly.

A new job as a temp EMT—emergency medical technician.

One would think that after all the moves and all the

fresh starts she'd made in her lifetime that *new* would be old hat to her by now, but truthfully she'd never quite gotten the hang of it.

The Pacific Ocean pounded the surf behind her as she got out of her car. The hot, salty June air brushed across her face as her nerves continued to dance. What was it her mother had said every time she'd uprooted them to follow yet another get-rich-quick scheme or new boyfriend or some other ridiculous notion?

It will be okay. You'll see.

And though her mother had been wrong about so many things, somehow it really had always been okay. Today would be no different. The azure sky held a single white puffy cloud hanging high over a dreamy sea dotted with whitecaps and a handful of sailboats. Three-foot waves hit the sand, splashing the pelicans fishing for their morning meal. Nice…if she had to make yet another new start, this didn't seem like such a bad way to go.

Hitching her bag up on her shoulder, Brooke started toward the station, a two-story brick-red structure with white trim and a yard filled with grass and wildflowers swaying in the breeze.

In the huge opened garage sat three fire trucks and an ambulance. One wall was lined with equipment such as hoses and ladders.

Surfboards leaned against the outside of the building. Oak trees dotted the edge of the property, and between the two largest, near the path to the front door, a man swung on a large hammock.

A man with broad shoulders, long legs and the unmistakable build of an athlete. His boots lay on the grass beneath him, as well as a discarded button-down shirt, leaving him in blue uniform pants slid just low enough on his hips to reveal a strip of black BVDs. His white T-shirt invited the general public to bite him. He had his hands clasped behind his head, and a large straw hat covered his face. His stillness suggested he was deeply asleep.

She slowed to a tiptoe, trying not to stare but failing. She was petite, and therefore constantly had to prove to people how strong she could be, but she'd bet he'd never had to prove anything; even from his prone position, he radiated strength and confidence. Of course that long, tough body didn't hurt, with all that aesthetically pleasing sinew defined even as he snoozed.

She envied the nap. She couldn't remember the last time she'd taken one. Or the last time she'd taken a moment to just lie on a hammock and soak up the sun.

Or even just to breathe, for that matter.

A lot of that came from being raised by a wild child of a mother, with little to no stability or security. And though Brooke had been on her own since high school, things hadn't changed much. She'd followed suit, living how she knew, moving around, bouncing from junior college to undergrad to working as an EMT, all in different cities. Hell, different states. Some habits died hard.

But she'd never landed in California before. She'd come to deal with her grandmother's estate, which included a great big old house and no cash to take care of the mortgage. Wasn't that just like an O'Brien.

It left Brooke with no choice but to sell the place off before it dragged her down in debt. Except she had to pack up some sixty-plus years of living first. And hell, maybe while the house was on the market, she could learn more about the grandma she'd never known.

In the meantime, she needed money for the immediates—like, say, eating—and the temp EMT position was for six weeks.

Perfect.

At least on the outside looking in, which was pretty much how she lived her life. Someday she'd like to change that. Someday she'd like to find her niche.

Find where she really belonged…

But for now, or at least the next six weeks, she belonged here. As she moved past the dozing firefighter, the sea breeze stirred her hair and tickled her nose. Then another gust of wind hit, knocking her back a step, and still the occupant of the hammock didn't move, breathing slow and deep, his chest rising and falling in rhythm. She kept tiptoeing past him, then pretty much undid all her careful stealth by sneezing. And not a dainty-girl sneeze, either.

The long body stirred, and so did something deep within her, which was so odd as to be almost unrecognizable.

Lust?

Huh. It'd been a while since she'd felt such instant heat for a guy, especially one whose face she hadn't even seen yet.

His hand reached up to tip off his hat, revealing short, sun-streaked brown hair. When he turned his head in her direction, she caught a quick flash of a face that definitely matched the body, and more of that stirring occurred. He'd been blessed by the gene-pool angels, and freezing on the spot, Brooke watched as two light green eyes focused, then offered a lazy smile. "Bless you," he said.

He had a voice to go with the rest of him—low, deep and melodic. Uh-oh. Lots more stirring and a rise of instantaneous heat, because, good Lord, if she'd thought him virile with his eyes closed, she needed a respirator to look at him now. "Sorry to wake you."

"No worries. I'm used to it. Besides, you're a much prettier sight than anything I was dreaming about."

They were just words but they brought a little zing to her good spots. Good spots she'd nearly let rust. *Whew.* Suddenly, she was actually beginning to sweat. If someone had asked her before this moment if she believed in lust at first sight, she'd have laughed. No, she needed more than hot sexiness in a guy, always had.

But she wasn't laughing now.

Wanting to hear him talk some more, she asked, "What were you dreaming about?"

"We responded to a fire last night and lost a kid."

Some of that overwhelming lust relegated itself to the background of her brain, replaced by something far more real to her than mere physical attraction. *Empathy.* She'd lost people, too, and it never stopped hurting. "I'm so sorry."

"Yeah. Me, too." Shifting his muscular, athletic body in the hammock so that he lay on his side facing her, he propped his head on his hand. "So let me guess. You're the latest EMT."

"Yes. Brooke O'Brien."

"Zach Thomas."

"Hi, Zach Thomas."

His eyes warmed to a simmer, and a matching heat came from deep in her belly. Holy smokes, could he see the steam escaping from her pores? It was so strange, her immediate reaction to him. Strange and unsettling. "What do you mean latest?"

"They've sent us six EMTs so far." He smiled without much mirth. "No, seven. Yeah, you're the seventh."

Okay, that didn't sound promising. "What's wrong with the job?"

"Besides crazy twelve-hour shifts for the glory of low pay and little or no recognition?" He let out a low laugh, and she found that the butterflies in her belly were dancing to a new tune now. Not nerves, but something far earthier.

"No one mentioned that I'm the seventh temp, or that they'd had any problem filling the position."

"Did I scare you off?"

"Did you want to?"

He lifted a shoulder, not breaking eye contact. "If you scare easily, then it'd be nice to know now."

A challenge, and more of that shocking, undeniable sexual zing.

Did he feel it? "I don't scare at all."

At that, something new came into his gaze. Approval, which she didn't need, to go along with that undeniable awareness of her as a woman.

She didn't need that, either, but damn, it was good to know she wasn't alone in this. Whatever this was. Since she wasn't ready to put a finger on it, she forced herself to stop looking at him. "I don't actually officially start until tomorrow, but the chief suggested that I come by, check the place out." And, she supposed, meet the crew, who, it sounded like, were tired of meeting people who didn't stick.

But she'd stick. At least for the six weeks she'd been hired for, because if she was anything, it was reliable.

"Would you like the tour?"

Yes, please, of your body. "No, don't get up," she said quickly when he started to do just that. "Really. I'll manage."

"Door's unlocked," he said, watching her, gaze steady.

"Great. I'll just…" *Try to stop staring at you.* Jeez, it'd been too long since she'd had sex. *Waaaay* too long. "Nice meeting you."

"How about I say the same if you're at work tomorrow?"

"I'll be here." She might be nearly drunk with lust but she knew that much. She would be there.

"Hope so." His light eyes held hers for another beat, and more uncomfortable little zings of heat ping-ponged through her.

Whew. Any more of this and she was going to need another application of deodorant this morning. "I will," she insisted. "I always follow through." She just didn't always grow roots. Okay, she never grew roots. Turning away, she let out a long breath and, hopefully, some of the sexual tension with it, and headed toward the door, which stood ajar. "Hello?"

Utter silence, broken only by a gurgling sound. The front room looked like a grown-up version of a frat house, not quite as neat and organized as the garage, but clean. There were two long comfy-looking sofas and several cushy chairs in beach colors that were well lived in. Shelves lined one wall, piled and stacked with a wide assortment of books, magazines and DVDs. On the floor sat a huge basket filled with flip-flops and bottles of suntan lotion. Another wall was lined with hooks, from which hung individual firefighter gear bags.

She could see the kitchen off to the right and a hallway to the left, but still no sign of life, which was odd—they couldn't all be off on calls, not with the rigs still out front. *"Hello?"*

Still nothing.

With a shrug, she headed toward the gurgling sound, which took her into the kitchen, and a coffeemaker, making away. "Who'd want coffee on a hot day?" she asked herself.

"A crew who's been up all night."

Turning around, she faced sexy firefighter Zach Thomas, and as potent as he'd been lying down, his hotness factor shot up exponentially now that he was standing, even with bed-head—or hammock-head—which was good news for him…and bad news for her.

Letting out a huge yawn, he covered his mouth, then grimaced. "Sorry."

He looked good even when yawning. She was so screwed. "Don't be."

He set down his boots and shirt and stretched. His T-shirt rose, giving her a quick peek at a set of lickable abs. He ran a hand over his hair, which only encouraged the short strands to riot in an effortlessly sexy way that might have been amusing if she hadn't been in danger of drooling.

She'd never been one to lose it for a guy in uniform, so she had no idea why now was any different, but *oh my*.

"We had seven calls last night," he explained. "Fires, an explosion in the sugar factory, a toxic-waste spill at the gas station on Fifth. You name it, we were at it, all night. None of us got more than an hour." Again he ran his hand over his already-standing-on-end hair. "We're wiped. Everyone's sleeping."

Beneath all that gorgeousness, true exhaustion lined his face, and suddenly Brooke saw him as a flesh-and-blood man. "I'm sorry I woke you. Especially after such a rough night."

He lifted another shoulder, not anywhere close to how irritated and frustrated she'd be if she'd had only an hour of sleep. "That's the way this job works. You wanted to meet the crew?"

"I'll come back."

"You want coffee first?"

She opened her mouth to say no thanks, but then she saw it in his gaze. His guard coming up. Here he was, overworked, the place obviously short-staffed, and in his eyes, she was just one in a long line of people that had flaked. That would flake. "You know, coffee would be great."

He turned to the cupboards while she took in the kitchen. The table was huge, with at least twelve chairs scattered around it. On the counter ran a line of mugs the length of the tile. "How many of you are stationed here?"

"We're on three rotating shifts, with only six firefighters and two EMTs each, which makes us…twenty-four? Down from thirty, thanks to some nasty cutbacks."

A medium-size station, then, but huge compared to the private ambulance company she'd last worked for, where there'd been only four on at all times.

She'd have to be far more social here than she was used to. The firefighters worked twenty-four-hour shifts to the EMTs' twelve, but it was still a lot of time together. She told herself that was a bonus, but really it just drove home that, once again, she was the new kid in class.

Zach eased over to the coffeepot. "Black, or jacked up?"

"Jacked up, please."

He reached for the sugar. Without her permission, her

eyes took themselves on a little tour, starting with those wide shoulders, that long, rangy torso, and a set of buns that—

He turned and, oh perfect, caught her staring.

At his butt.

Arching a brow, he leaned back against the counter while she did her best imitation of a ceiling tile. When she couldn't stand the silence and finally took a peek at him, he was handing her the mug of coffee, his eyes amused.

"Thanks," she managed.

"You're not from around here." He poured another mug for himself.

All her life she hadn't been "from around here," so that was nothing new. Getting caught staring at a guy's ass? That was new. New and very uncomfortable. "Is that a requirement?"

"Ah, and a little defensive," he said easily. "You look new to Santa Rey, that's all."

"And you know that because…?"

"Because of your skin." Reaching out, he stroked a finger over her cheek, and instantly she felt as if all her happy spots sparked to life. She sucked in a breath.

So did he.

After a pause, he pulled his finger back. "Huh."

Yeah, huh.

"You're pale," he said. "That's what I meant. You're obviously not from a beach town."

Okay, so they weren't going to discuss it. "I'm just careful, is all."

Zach nodded slowly. "I didn't mean to ruffle you."

Even though he was clearly ruffled, too. He slid his feet into his boots, leaving them unlaced as he set down his coffee and shrugged into his uniform shirt.

Maybe he hadn't meant to ruffle her, but that's exactly what he'd done, was still doing just by breathing. "I'm a big fan of sunscreen."

With a nod, he came close again, his gaze touching over her features. "It was a compliment. You have gorgeous skin, all creamy smooth." Again, he stroked a finger over her cheek, and like before, she felt the touch in a whole bunch of places that had no business feeling anything.

He was ruffling her again. Big-time ruffling going on, from her brain cells to all her erogenous zones, of which she had far more than she remembered.

"Back East?" he guessed.

"Massachusetts." Brooke was trying not to react to the fact that he was in her personal bubble, or that she was enjoying the invasion. "You, uh…" She wagged her finger toward his shirt, still partially opened over the invitation to bite him, which she suddenly wanted to do. "Didn't finish buttoning."

"You distracted me."

Yeah. A mutual problem, apparently. This close, he seemed even taller and broader, and now his surfer good looks were only exaggerated by the firefighter uniform. "Are the surfboards outside yours?"

"Why?" He flashed a smile that must have slayed female hearts across the land. It certainly slayed hers. "Because I look like a surfer?"

"Yes."

"Do you surf?"

"I've never tried," she admitted. "I'm not sure it'd be a good idea."

"Why?"

"I'm…" She paused, not exactly relishing telling this gorgeous specimen of a man her faults.

"A little uptight?" he guessed, then looked her over. "Maybe even a little bit of a perfectionist?"

"Are you suggesting I'm anal? Because I'm not."

He just kept looking at her, a little amused, and she caved like a cheap suitcase. "Okay, I am. What gave me away?"

"The hair."

Which she had in a neat braid. "Keeps it out of my way."

"Smart. And the ironed cargoes?"

She slid her hands into her pockets. "So I hate wrinkles."

A smile tugged at the corners of his mouth. "Yeah, wrinkles are a bitch."

Damn it. He was gorgeous *and* perceptive. "Fine. I'm a lot anal."

He let out another slow and easy grin.

And something within her began a slow and easy burn.

Oh, this wasn't good. It was the opposite of good. "Maybe I should just come back—"

But before she could finish that thought, a loud bell clanged, and in the blink of an eye the surfer firefighter went from laid-back and easygoing to tense and alert.

"Units two and three, respond to 3640 Rebecca Avenue," said a disembodied voice from the loudspeaker.

"That's me." Zach set down his mug as movement came from down the hall.

People began filing into the front room in various stages of readiness, most of them guys—really hot guys, Brooke couldn't help but notice—half of them pulling on clothes, some shoving on shoes, others giving orders to others. All looked exhausted, and somewhat out of sorts. Having been up all night, they couldn't be thrilled at having to move out now, but she still expected someone to ask about her, or even acknowledge her, but no one did.

"Mary's temp is here," Zach said into the general chaos. "Brooke O'Brien, everyone."

People gave a quick wave, one or two even quicker smiles, and kept moving. Zach squeezed her shoulder as he headed to the door, once again a simple touch from him giving her a jolt. "See you around, New Hire Number Seven." And just like that, he was gone.

They were all gone.

Yeah. Definitely still the new kid.

2

BROOKE SPENT that night walking through the three-story Victorian her grandmother had so unexpectedly left her, marveling that it was in her name now. She'd never met Lucille O'Brien, who'd been estranged from her only child, Brooke's mother, Karen, so it'd been a shock to everyone when Brooke had been contacted by an attorney and given the details of Lucille's will.

As she'd been warned by the attorney, every room was indeed filled to the brim with…stuff. For Brooke, for whom everything she owned could fit into her car, this accumulation of stuff boggled the mind. All of it would have to go in order to sell the house, but she didn't know where to start. Her mother had been no help, wanting nothing to do with any of it, not even willing to come West to look.

But Brooke was glad she'd come. If nothing else, being in Santa Rey, experiencing that inexplicably over-the-top attraction to Zach, staying here in the only place her family had any history at all, gave her a sense that she might actually have a shot at things she'd never dared dream about before.

She finally decided to go top to bottom and headed to the attic. There she went to the first pile she came to and found a stack of photo boxes that unexpectedly snagged her by the throat. The way she'd grown up hadn't allowed for much sentimentality. None of her few belongings included keepsakes like photos. She'd told herself over the years that it didn't matter. She *liked* to be sentiment light.

But flipping through boxes and boxes of pictures, she realized that was only because she hadn't known any different. Karen and Lucy hadn't spoken in years, since back when Brooke had been a baby, so she hadn't known her grandmother, or how the woman felt about her. But some of the pictures were from the early 1900s and continued through her grandmother's entire life, enthralling Brooke in a way she hadn't expected.

She had a past, and flipping through it made her feel good, and also sad for all she didn't know. She and her mother weren't close. In fact, Karen lived in Ohio at the moment, with an artist and wasn't in touch often, but now Brooke wished she could just pick up a phone and share this experience.

That she had anyone to pick up a phone and call…

She fell asleep just like that, surrounded by her past, only to wake with a jerk, the sun slanting in the small window high above her. She had two pictures stuck to one cheek, drool on the other. She'd been dreaming about the big house, filled with memories of her own making.

Was that what she secretly wished for? For this house to represent her roots?

Was that what she needed to feed her own happiness?

She glanced at her watch and then panicked. Tossing off the dream and the photos, she raced through her morning routine, barely getting a shower before rushing out the door, desperate not to be late on her first day at work.

The hammock by the firehouse was empty, and she ignored the little twinge of disappointment at not getting to gawk at Zach again. Not that she was going to gawk. Nope, she was going to be one hundred percent professional. And with that, she stepped inside.

"Well, look at you. You really came back."

Danger, danger...sexy firefighter alert. Slowly she turned and looked at him, thinking, *Please don't be as hot as I remember, please don't be as hot as I remember—*

Shit.

He was as hot as she remembered. He didn't look tired this morning. Instead, the corners of his mouth were turned up, and his eyes—cheerful and wide-awake—slid over her, making her very aware of the fact that while she might have a little crush going, it was most definitely, absolutely, a two-way thing.

Which didn't help at all.

"Guys," he called out over his shoulder. "She's here."

"Number Seven showed?" This from a tall, dark and extremely drool-worthy firefighter in the doorway to the kitchen.

"Meet Aidan," Zach said to Brooke. "He dated New Hire Number Two and she never came back, so he has orders to stay clear."

"Hey, I didn't plan on the shellfish giving her food poisoning," Aidan said in his own defense. "But just in case..." He flashed a smile at Brooke, a killer smile that rivaled Zach's. "We'd better not go out for shellfish."

Several more men crowded into the hallway to take a look. Yeah, they really did make them good-looking here. Must be the fresh sea air. "Hi," she said, waving. "Brooke O'Brien."

The bell rang, and everyone groaned, their greeting getting lost as they headed for their gear.

"Aidan and I roll together," Zach said, stepping into his boots. "With Cristina and Blake." He gestured to two additional firefighters, the first a tough-looking beautiful blond woman who smiled, the other, male, tall and lanky, not smiling.

Zach shook his head. "Or, as we call Blake, Eeyore."

Okay. Brooke wasn't smiling, either, so she put one on now, but it was too late; they'd turned away.

"You're with Dustin," Zach called back.

Dustin, who looked like Harry Potter The Grown-Up Years, complete with glasses, raised his hand. "We're the two EMTs on this shift. Nice to meet you. Hope you orientate fast."

She hoped so, too.

Dustin gestured to the door, nodding to the two firefighters not moving. "This is Sam and Eddie. Their rig wasn't called, so they get to stay here and watch *Oprah* and eat bonbons."

They took the ribbing with a collective flip of their middle fingers, then vanished back down the hall.

"Actually, they're scheduled to go to the middle school on Ninth this morning and give a fire safety and prevention speech to the kids," Dustin told her with a grin. "They'll eat their bonbons later. Let's hit it, New Hire Seven. It's a Code Calico."

"Code Calico?"

But he was already moving to the door that led directly to the garage and the rigs.

Cristina brushed past Brooke and set her mug in the sink. "Good luck."

"Am I going to need it?"

"With Dustin, our resident McDweeb? Oh, yeah, you're going to need it."

"What's a Code Calico?"

Cristina merely laughed, which did nothing to ease Brooke's nerves.

Blake poked his head back in the door. He'd pulled on his outer fire gear, which looked slightly too big on his very lean form. "Hey, New Hire. Hit it means hit it."

So she did what was expected of her—she hit it. Dustin drove, while she took the shotgun position. "So really, what's a Code Calico?"

Dustin navigated the streets with a familiar sort of ease that told her he knew what he was doing, not even glancing at the GPS system. "Want to take it?"

"Take it?"

"Be point on the call." He glanced at her. "The one in charge."

She sensed it was a test. She aced tests, always had. That was the analness in her, she supposed. "Sure."

He pushed up his glasses and nodded, but she'd have sworn his lips twitched.

Huh. Definitely missing something.

When they pulled onto a wide, affluent, oak-lined street, she hopped out and opened the back doors of the rig.

"Gurney's not necessary on this one," Dustin told her.

Behind the ambulance came the fire truck. Zach and the others appeared, smiling.

Why were they all smiling?

Before she could dwell on that, from between the two trucks came an old woman, yelling and waving her cane. "Hurry! Hurry before Cecile falls!"

The panic in her voice was real, and Brooke's heart raced just as Dustin nudged her forward, whispering in her ear, "All yours."

This was the job, and suddenly in her element, her nerves took a backseat. Here, she could help; here, she could run the show. "It's okay, ma'am. We're here now."

"Well, then, get to it! Get my Cecile!"

"Where is she? In the house?"

"No!" She looked very shaky and not a little off her rocker, so Brooke tried to steer her to the curb to sit down, but she wasn't having it.

"I'm not sitting anywhere! Not until you get Cecile!"

"Okay, just tell me where she is and I'll—"

"Oh, good Lord!" The woman blinked through her thick-rimmed glasses, taking a quick look at the others, who stood back, watching. "She's another new hire, isn't she?"

"Yes," Brooke said. "But—"

"What number are you?"

Brooke sighed. "Seven."

"Well, get a move on, New Hire Number Seven! Save my Cecile!"

"I'm trying, ma'am. What's your name?"

"Phyllis, but Cecile—"

"Right. Needs my help. Where is she?"

"That's what I'm trying to tell you!" The woman jerked her cane upward, to a huge tree in front of them. Waaaay up in that tree, on a branch stretched out over their heads, perched a cat.

A big, fat cat, plaintively wailing away.

Brooke turned and eyeballed Dustin, who seemed to be fascinated by his own feet, and that's when she got it. She was going through some ridiculously juvenile rite of passage. "I'm beginning to see how they got to number seven." Good thing she was used to being the newbie, because she hadn't been kidding Zach yesterday. Little scared her, and certainly not a damn cat in a damn tree.

"Hurry up!" Phyllis demanded. "Before she falls!"

"I'll get her." Zach had separated from the others and walked toward the tree.

Oh, no.

Hell, no.

They'd wanted to see her do this, they were absolutely going to see her do this.

"Brooke—"

"No." She kept her eyes on Phyllis. "Cecile is a cat," she clarified, because there was no sense in making a total and complete fool of herself if it wasn't absolutely necessary.

"Yes," Phyllis verified.

Okay, it was going to be absolutely necessary. Damn, she hated that.

By now, Barbie Firefighter Cristina was out-and-out grinning. Cutie Firefighter Aidan was smiling. Harry Potter look-alike Dustin was, too. Not Eeyore, though. Nope, Blake was far more serious than the others, she could already tell, though she'd have sworn there was some amusement shining in his gaze.

Zach was either wiser, or maybe he simply had more control, but his lips weren't curved as he watched her. Quiet. Aware. Speculative.

Sexy as hell, damn him. Fine. Seemed she had a lot to prove to everyone. Well, she was good at that, too, and she stepped toward the tree.

"Brooke—"

She put a finger in his face, signaling Don't You Dare, and something flashed in his eyes.

Respect? Yeah, but something else, too, something much more base, which would have most definitely set off one of their trademark chain reactions of sparks along her central nervous system, if she hadn't been about to climb a damn tree. "I can do this," she said.

His eyes approved, and even though she didn't want it to, that approval washed through her.

So did that sizzling heat they had going on.

Oh, he was good. With that charisma oozing from his every pore, he could no doubt charm the panties off just about any woman.

But though it had been a while since anyone had charmed Brooke's panties off, she wasn't just any woman.

Reminding herself of that, she stepped toward the tree.

3

ZACH WATCHED how Brooke handled herself and something inside him reacted. He didn't know her, not yet, not really, other than that they had some serious almost chemical-like attraction going, but she was crew, and as such, she was family.

Except he felt decidedly un-family-like toward her. Nope, nothing in him looking at her felt brotherly.

Not one little bit.

The gang was being hard on her, there was no doubt of that, but he'd seen many new hires hazed over the years—six in the past few weeks—and it had never bothered him.

Until now. This bothered him. *She* bothered him, in a surprising way. A man-to-woman way, though that wasn't the surprise. It was that he felt it here, at work.

People came in and out of his life on a daily basis. It was the nature of the beast, that beast being fire. Every day he dealt with the destruction it caused, and what it did to people's existence. Hell, he'd even experienced it in the most personal way one could, when he'd lost his own parents to a tragic fire. He coped by knowing he made a difference, that he helped keep that beast back when he could.

What also helped were the constants in his life, and since the loss of his mom and dad at age ten, those constants were his crew. Aidan, his partner and brother of his heart. Eddie and Sam, fellow surfers. Dustin, resident clown, a guy who gave one hundred percent of himself, always, which usually landed him in Heartbreak City. Blake, whom he'd gone to high school with and who'd lost his firefighting partner Lynn in a tragic fire last year, a guy who'd give a perfect stranger the heavy yellow jacket off his back. Even Cristina, a woman in a man's world, who was willing to kick anyone's ass to show she belonged in it. All of them held a piece of Zach's heart.

For better, for worse, through thick and thin, they were each other's one true, solid foundation. They meant everything to him.

But the emergency community they lived in was a lot like the cozy little town of Santa Rey itself—small and quirky, no secrets need apply. Everyone knew that the constant gossip and ribbing between the crew members acted as stress relief from a job that had an element of danger every time they went out. Zach had always considered it harmless. But looking at it from Brooke's perspective, that ribbing must feel like mockery.

She dropped her bag to the ground and walked to the tree.

She was going to climb it for the cat. And hell if that didn't do something for him. He didn't interfere—she was Dustin's partner, not his—but he wanted to. The chief would have a coronary, of course, but the chief wasn't there throwing the rule book around as he liked to do. Zach wasn't much for rules or restrictions, himself, or for drawing lines in the sand—which hadn't helped his career any. Nor did he make a habit of stretching his emotional wings and adding personal ties to his life. How many women had told him over the years that he wouldn't know a real relationship if it bit him on the ass?

Too many to count.

And yet he felt an emotional tie now, watching Brooke simply do her job. It shouldn't have been sexy, but it was. *She* was sexy, even in the regulation EMT uniform of dark blue trousers and a white button-down shirt, with a Santa Rey EMT vest over the top, the outfit made complete by the required steel-toed boots.

She made him hot. He thought maybe it was the perfectly folded-back sleeves and careful hair twist that got him. Her hair was gorgeous, a shiny strawberry blond, her coloring as fair as her hair dictated. He knew after any time in the sun—and in Santa Rey, sun was the only weather they got—she'd probably freckle across that nose she liked to tip up to nosebleed heights. She was petite, small-boned, even fragile-looking, and yet he'd bet his last dollar she was strong as hell, strong enough for that tree.

She looked up at the lowest branch, utter concentration on her face. A face that showed her emotions, probably whether she wanted it to or not. It was those wide, expressive baby-blue eyes, he knew. They completely slayed him.

She put her hands on the trunk of the tree and gave it a shake, testing it. Nodding to herself, still eyeing the cat as if she'd rather be facing a victim who was bleeding out than the howling feline on the branch twenty feet above her, she drew a deep breath.

Unbelievable. She was slightly anal, slightly obsessive and more than slightly adorable.

And she had guts. He liked that. He liked her. She was

taking his mind off his frustration over the Hill Street fire and Tommy's investigation. But while his career was shaky at the moment, hers was not, and she was going to climb that damn tree if no one stopped her. "Dustin."

Cristina shushed him. Blake, the one of them who couldn't stand to see anything suffer, even before losing Lynn last year, shot her an annoyed look. Zach leaned toward Dustin. "Stop her."

"On it." The EMT stepped forward and put his hand on Brooke's shoulder, saying something that Zach couldn't quite catch, though he had no problem reading her expression.

Relief that she didn't really have to climb the tree.

Embarrassment that she'd let them all fool her.

And a flash of a temper that made him smile. Good. She might be reserved, but she wasn't a doormat.

Aidan grabbed the ladder. Zach helped him. As he passed a brooding Brooke, their eyes met before he climbed the ladder to reach Cecile.

Yeah, quiet and reserved, maybe, but also a little pissed. So was Cecile, but she was one female he could soothe, at least, and when he brought the cat to Phyllis, he had to smile.

Brooke had the older woman sitting on the curb and was attempting to check her vitals, which Phyllis didn't appear to appreciate.

"Ma'am," Brooke said, "you have an elevated blood pressure."

"Well, of course I do. I'm eighty-eight."

Brooke lifted her stethoscope, but Phyllis pushed it away. "I don't need—Cecile! Give me my baby, Zachie!"

Blowing a loose strand of hair from her face, Brooke gave Zach a look. *"Zachie?"*

"Small town." With a half-embarrassed shrug, he handed the cat to Phyllis.

"I used to change his diapers," Phyllis told her, and patted Zach's cheek with fingers gnarled by arthritis. "You're a good boy. Your mother would be so proud of you."

He'd found it best not to respond to these types of statements from Phyllis, because if he did, she'd keep him talking about his family forever, and he didn't like to talk about them. He thought about them every day, and that was enough. "I thought we decided you were going to keep Cecile inside."

"No, *you* decided, but she hates being cooped up." She nuzzled the cat. "So how's all your ladies, Zachie? Still falling at your feet?"

Brooke arched a brow but Zach just smiled. "You're my number-one lady, Phyllis, you know that." Her color wasn't great, plus her breathing was off, which worried him. She'd probably forgotten to pick up her meds again. He crouched at her side and took her hand. "You're taking your pills, right?"

She bent her head to Cecile's, her blue hair bouncing in the breeze. "Oh, well. You know."

With a sigh, he reached for Brooke's blood pressure cuff. "May I?"

Their fingers brushed as she put it in his hand, and again he felt that electric current zing him, but as hot as that little zap was, he didn't take his gaze off Phyllis. "You know the drill," he said, gently wrapping the cuff around her arm as above him he heard Brooke say to Dustin, "So did I pass the test?"

"Yep. Nice job, New Hire Seven."

"You've got to keep the cat inside," Zach said to

Phyllis, handing back the blood pressure cuff to Brooke, making sure to touch her, testing their connection. Yep, still there. "Cecile's not safe out here, Phyllis."

"She's safe now."

"Yes." With effort, he shifted his mind off Brooke and focused on Phyllis. "We have a new chief."

"Yes, of course. Allan Stone. Santa Rey born and raised, back from Chicago to do good in his hometown. I read all about him in the paper."

Everything was in the Santa Rey paper. Not that Zach needed to read it. Not when he and the chief were becoming intimately familiar with each other; every time Zach put his nose into Tommy's business regarding the arsons, he got some personal one-on-one time in the chief's office. "After all he saw in Chicago, he's not going to think this qualifies as an emergency."

"But it was an emergency."

"I'm sorry, Phyllis."

"Yes." The older woman sighed. "I know. I'm old, not senile. I get it." She lovingly stroked the cat, who sprawled in her lap, purring loudly enough to wake the dead. "It's just that Cecile loves the great outdoors. And you always come—"

Seemed his heart was going to get tugged on plenty today. "That's my point. We can't always come. If we're here when there's an emergency, then someone else might go without our help. I know you don't want that to happen."

"No, of course not." She hugged the cat hard. "You're right. I'm sorry."

"No apologies necessary." He scratched the cat behind her ornery ears and rose to leave.

Brooke blocked his path. She still held her stethoscope and blood pressure cuff, looking sweetly professional while she tried to maintain her composure, but her annoyance at being played was clear.

"I'd like to talk to you," she said primly.

He enjoyed that, too, the way she sounded so prissy while looking so damn hot. So put together, so on top of everything, which perversely made him want to rumple her up. Preferably the naked, hot and sweaty kind of rumpled. "Talk? Or bite my head off?"

"I don't bite."

"Shame." Passing her, he headed back to his rig to help Aidan put away the ladder. But she wasn't done with him yet, and followed.

"I nearly climbed that tree, Zach. Without the benefit of the ladder, I might add."

Aidan shot Zach a look that said Good Luck, Buddy and moved out of their way. Zach turned to face a fuming Brooke. "No one was going to let you climb that tree."

"Really? Because I think that the crew thinks I was sent here to amuse them."

"You have to understand, you're the seventh EMT—"

"To walk out, yeah yeah, got it. But I'm not going to walk out. I'm not."

"I believe you."

"You do?"

He smiled at her surprise. "I do. And I was never going to let you climb that tree, Brooke. Never."

She stared at him for a long, silent beat. "Is your word supposed to mean something?"

He was a lot of things, but a liar was not one of them. Not that she could possibly know that about him yet. "Hopefully it will come to mean something."

She continued to look at him for another long moment, then turned and walked away with a quiet sense of dignity that made him feel like an ass even though, technically, he'd done nothing wrong.

OVER THE NEXT FEW DAYS the calls came nonstop, accompanying a heat wave that had everyone at the firehouse on edge, Zach included. If they'd had the staff that they used to, things would have been okay, but they didn't. So they ran their asses off in oppressive temperatures with no downtime, while the higher-ups got to sit in air-conditioned offices.

By the end of the week, they were all exhausted.

"Crazy," Cristina muttered on the third straight day of record-high temperatures *and* calls. "It's like with the heat wave came a stupid wave."

They were all in the kitchen, gulping down icy drinks and standing in front of the opened freezer, vying for space and ice cubes. Cristina rubbed an ice cube across her chest, then gave poor Dustin the evil eye for staring at her damp breasts.

Zach didn't blame Dustin for looking; the view was mighty nice. He did worry about the dreamy look in the EMT's eyes. Dustin tended to put his heart on the line for every single woman he met, which left him open to plenty of heartbreak. If Cristina caught that puppy-dog look, she'd chew him up and spit him out. Instead, she elbowed everyone back and took the front-and-center spot for herself.

"You forgot to take your pill this morning," Blake told her, not looking at her chest like everyone else but nudging her out of the way so he could get in closer.

"I'm not on the pill," Cristina said.

"Not that pill. Your nice pill."

Dustin snorted and Cristina glared at him, zapping the smile off his face.

Zach cleared some space for Brooke to get in closer, and she sent him a smile that zapped him as sure as Cristina had zapped Dustin, but in another area entirely.

He wished she was rubbing an ice cube on her chest. He maneuvered himself right next to her. Their arms bumped, their legs brushed and every nerve ending went on high alert.

The bell rang, and with a collective groan, they all scattered. It was exhausting, and *he* was seasoned, as was the crew. He could only imagine how Brooke felt. If he'd had time to breathe, he'd have asked her.

As it was, they couldn't do much more than glance at each other, because between the multitude of calls, they still had the maintaining and keeping up of the station and vehicles, not to mention their required physical training.

But he did glance at her.

Plenty.

And she glanced back. She appeared to hold up under pressure extremely well; even when everyone else looked hot, sweaty and irritated, she never did. Look sweaty and irritated, that is.

Hot? That she most definitely looked.

It'd been a long time since he'd flirted so slowly with a woman like this, over days, mostly without words. A very long time, and he'd forgotten how arousing it could be. He figured if they had to pass each other one more time without taking it to the next step—and he had plenty of ideas on what that next step should be, all involving touching and stripping and nakedness, lots of nakedness—they'd both go up in flames.

One late afternoon a week and a half into Brooke's employment, he headed toward her to see about that whole thing, but of course, the bell rang.

It was a kitchen fire, with a man down. Zach and Aidan were first on scene, with Dustin and Brooke pulling in right behind them in front of a small house that sat on a high bluff overlooking the ocean. By the time they got inside, the fire had been extinguished by the supposedly downed man himself, who was breathing like a lunatic and looked to be in the throes of a panic attack. Zach and Aidan checked to make sure the doused fire couldn't flare up and then began mop-up while Dustin tried to get the guy to sit, but he wasn't having it.

"No." Chest heaving, covered in soot, he pointed at Brooke. "I want her. The chick paramedic."

Everyone looked at Brooke. For some reason, she looked at Zach. He wanted to think it was because they'd been looking at each other silently for days, building an odd sense of anticipation for…something, but probably it was simply that he'd been the first person she'd met here.

"I'm an EMT," she told the victim. "Not a paramedic."

"I don't care." The guy was gasping for air, clutching at his chest. "It's you or nothing."

HER OR NOTHING. Brooke could honestly say that she'd never heard that sentence before, at least directed at her. She looked at the crew around her, all of whom were looking at her, perfectly willing and accepting of her taking over.

And in that moment, she knew. They might tease her

and call her New Hire, but the truth was, they treated her as a part of their team, a capable, smart part of their team, and she appreciated that. "What's your name?"

"Carl."

"Okay, Carl. Let's sit."

"I'm better standing. Listen, I was just cooking eggs, but then the pan caught fire."

"It's okay," Brooke assured him. "The fire's out now. Let's worry about you."

"I have a problem."

Yes, he did. He was pale, clammy and sweating profusely. "Let's work on that problem."

"It's, uh, a big one. It won't go away." Still breathing heavy, the guy looked down at his fly. "If you know what I mean."

Everyone stopped working on the kitchen mop-up and looked at the guy's zipper, and Brooke did the same.

He was erect.

She glanced at the guys. Dustin pushed up his glasses. Aidan busied himself with the cleanup. Zach rubbed his jaw and met Brooke's gaze, his own saying that he'd seen it all, but not this.

Carl shoved his fingers through his hair, still trying to catch his breath. "See, I was supposed to have this hot date last night, but Mr. Winky wasn't working. So I took a vitamin V."

"Vitamin V?" Brooke pulled out a chair and firmly but gently pressed him into it. "What's vitamin V?"

"Viagra."

Brooke processed that information while Carl stared down at his lap with a mixture of pride and bafflement. "It worked, too. A little too well."

"Okay." Brooke opened her bag and began to check his vitals, carefully not looking at the guy's zipper again.

"So…can you fix this? I've never had a twelve-hour case of blue balls before. Could it…kill me?"

"No one's dying today." Behind her, Dustin was checking in with the hospital, as was protocol. From the victim she took the basics: name, age, weight, etc. Dustin set down his radio and turned to her. "We have a few questions."

"Not you," Carl said, shaking his head. *"Her."*

"Right." Dustin wrote something down and pushed the piece of paper toward Brooke. It was the questions the E.R. doctor wanted answered. She paused, tucking a non-existent stray piece of hair behind her ear while she tried to figure out how to do this and keep Carl's dignity, not to mention her own. "Carl? How many Viagras did you take?"

"Oh. Um." He looked away, catching Aidan's and Zach's eye. "Just the one."

Brooke gave him a long look. She was not a pushover, not even close. "One?"

"Okay, two."

"Are you sure?"

Mr. Vitamin V caved. "Four. Okay? I took four. I really wanted to do this." Still breathing unsteadily, he put his hand on his heart. "Am I going to have a heart attack? Because I feel like I'm having a heart attack."

Brooke was waiting on Dustin, who was talking to the E.R. about the four pills. "Just hang tight for a second."

"Hanging tight. Or at least my boys are." He smiled feebly at his joke. "Do I have to go to the hospital?"

"Finding that out now." She did her best not to squirm, extremely aware of all the eyes on her, especially Zach's, as Dustin gave her another piece of paper, which she read. *Oh, boy.* "Carl, when did you last have sex?"

Carl blinked. "When did I last have sex? Are you kidding me? That's why I took the pills in the first place!"

Again Brooke accidentally met Zach's gaze. He was cool, calm, and not showing a thing, but she felt her own face heat. If she had to answer this question, she'd have to admit that she couldn't even remember. "We need to know when you last ejaculated."

"Oh." Carl let out a long breath. "Jesus. Yesterday. In the shower."

Nodding, she made the note.

"Twice."

Brooke dropped her pen.

"That's normal, right?" He looked at Aidan, Dustin and then Zach for affirmation. "Back me up here, guys. It's just what we do, right?"

Aidan got really busy, fast.

Dustin scribbled on his notepad.

Zach just raised a brow.

"Damn it!" Carl slapped his hands on the table. "Don't you guys leave me out here hanging alone! Tell her."

Dustin sighed, then after a hesitation, nodded.

Aidan, too.

Brooke looked at Zach, who met her gaze evenly, not looking away, neither embarrassed nor self-conscious as he nodded, as well.

Carl was waiting for her next question, but she couldn't stop staring at Zach, couldn't stop picturing him—

Oh, perfect. And here came the blush.

Dustin nudged her and she jumped, jerking her gaze off Zach.

"Really, it's what guys do," Carl was still saying.

It was what guys did.

Drive her crazy.

They made the decision to transport, and while loading the patient in the small kitchen, Brooke bumped into Zach. She looked into his face, feeling hers heat, watching him smile as if he knew what she was thinking.

It's what guys do...

She moved past him but their arms touched, and damn if she didn't feel her stomach quiver. Because their arms touched. How ridiculous was that? If he ever touched her in a sexual way, she'd probably come before he even got her clothes off.

"You okay?" he murmured. "You're looking at me funny."

"Me?" Her voice was as high as Mickey Mouse. "No. Not at all." *I was looking at you like I wanted to gobble you up for my next meal, that's all.*

He cocked his head and studied her a moment. "Sure?"

"Sure." Liar, liar...

4

"HEY, NEW HIRE SEVEN," Cristina said several days later, the next time she saw Brooke. "Any more Viagra calls?"

Brooke looked over as Firefighter Barbie entered the fire station living room grinning from ear to ear. "Brooke. My name is Brooke."

"So. You ever have a patient with a perma-boner before?"

"No. That was a new one," Brooke admitted.

"At least you didn't have to climb a tree to get to him, huh?"

"At least he was human."

Cristina laughed and walked past Blake, who was on the computer, and affectionately rumpled his hair. "You get the message that your sister called?"

"Yep, thanks."

"Kenzie sounds good. I saw her on *Entertainment Tonight* last night, she was being interviewed about being nominated for a daytime Emmy for her soap."

"I taped it."

"We still all having dinner tonight, right?"

"Yep."

Brooke knew that they did that a lot, got together. All of them. They'd asked her to join them weeks ago, on her first night, but she had been anxious to get started packing up her grandma's house. Now that she'd been doing that for two weeks, she'd love to be included, but didn't know how to ask.

A lifelong problem—not knowing how to belong. But for the first time in her life, she wanted to. She didn't know if it was her grandmother's house with all that family history, or the way she yearned and burned for Zach at night, or just wanting more for herself from life, but she wanted to be a part of this team. A part of their family. At least for the month she had left. Then, when she did go, she'd have these memories. She'd have her own history to look back on and remember.

Cristina leaned over Blake's shoulder. "Got anything good today, Eeyore?"

Blake pulled open a drawer and held out a candy bar. "Careful," he warned. "I rigged it. The person who eats that is going to turn sweet."

"Not a chance."

With a sigh, Blake went back to the computer.

Brooke headed into the garage to restock their rig as end-of-shift protocol dictated. And then, blessedly, she was off the clock. Stepping outside, she was immediately hit by a sucker punch to the low belly area—not by the hot, salty summer air, but by good old-fashioned lust.

Zach stood on the bumper of the truck, hose in hand, leaning over his rig, squirting down the windows. Stripped to the waist, his skin glistened with a light sweat. She broke into a sweat, too, just from looking at him.

His back was sleek, smooth and sinewy, and improving the already fantastic view was the fact that his pants had slid low enough to once again reveal a strip of BVDs, blue today. His every muscle bunched and unbunched as he moved, hypnotizing her, fusing her to the spot. She didn't mean to keep staring, she really didn't, but was unable to help herself as she eyed his sun-streaked hair, his rock-solid and ready-for-action body, all corded bulk honed to a fine edge, topped with so much testosterone she could hardly breathe. He looked like the perennial surfer boy all grown up—and it hit her.

This might be more than a crush.

"If you come help, you can get a better view."

Oh, for God's sake. She jerked her gaze off him and pretended to search her purse for her keys while silently berating herself. "I'm sorry, I—"

"Are you kidding? A pretty woman looks at me, and she's sorry?"

"I wasn't looking—"

Tossing aside his hose, he lithely hopped down from the rig and came closer, letting out that damn slow, sexy smile of his. "Anal, uptight *and* a liar?"

"Okay, so I was looking." She crossed her arms and tried not to look at his chest but it was right in front of her, drawing her eyes. "But I didn't *want* to be looking."

With a soft laugh, he turned the tables, letting his gaze slowly run over her, from her hair to her toes and then back up again, stopping at a few spots that happily leaped to hopeful attention.

"Stop it." God, was that her voice, all cartoony-light and breathless? "What are you doing?"

"Looking," he murmured, mocking her. "And I wanted to."

"Okay, you know what? You need a damn shirt. And I'm going now."

Leaning back against the rig, he smiled, and damn

if it didn't short-circuit her wires. "Have anything special planned for your days off?" he asked. "Visiting friends, family?"

No. Fantasizing about you...

Unacceptable answer. She'd be working on the house. The house that she was beginning to wish was hers in more than name, because being there reminded her of exactly how rootlessly she'd lived her life, and how much she'd like to change that. Going through decades of family history had brought it home for her. It was exhausting, almost gut-wrenching, but also exhilarating.

And honestly? Flirting with Zach was the same.

But no matter what the house represented to her, no matter what someone like Zach could represent to her, she still didn't know how to get there.

How to belong. "I don't have either friends or family here."

"Everyone back East?"

She hated this part. Telling people about herself, getting unwanted sympathy. "My mother's in Ohio. I'm an only child. And I haven't made any friends here yet."

He didn't dwell or give her any sympathy. "I thought we were friends."

She gave him a look.

"Aren't we?"

"I don't know."

"Let's do something, then, and you can decide."

"I can't. I'm closing up my grandmother's house before it sells, and I've only got a month left in town."

"You think you'll be able to leave Santa Rey without falling in love with it? Or the people?"

She looked into his eyes, wishing for a witty response.

But the truth was, she fell a little bit more for her grandma's house every single night she slept there. "I don't know."

"Do you know how you feel about surfing?"

"I'm pretty uncoordinated."

"I'm a good teacher."

Uh-huh. She bet he was.

"Come on, say yes. I'm betting you don't take enough downtime."

"I take lots."

He arched a brow, and she let out a breath. "Okay, so I don't."

"Is that because you like to be so busy your head spins, or because you don't know how to relax?"

"Is there an option number three?"

"You work a stressful job."

"So?"

"So…" He smiled. "Maybe you should let that hair down and just be wild and free once in a while."

"Wild and free. Is that what you do?"

"When I can."

She hadn't expected him to admit it, and she ran out of words, especially because he was still standing there with no shirt on.

"Not your thing, I take it," he said. "Letting loose."

"I've never thought about it." Okay, she'd thought about it. "I'm not sure how to…let loose," she admitted, going to tuck her hair behind her ears. But he shifted closer and caught her fingers in his.

That electric current hummed between them. He looked at their joined hands and then into her eyes. "Maybe it's time to think about it," he said silkily and stroked a finger over the tip of her ear, causing a long set of shivers to race down her spine. Then, with a look that singed her skin, he walked off.

She managed, barely, not to let her knees give and sit right there on the ground. He wanted her to relax? Ha! So not likely, and not just because he wound her up in ways she hadn't anticipated. Relaxing, getting wild and free, those were all alien concepts for her. No matter what her secret desires were, she had responsibilities, always had. She didn't have time for letting loose.

But, as he'd suggested, she thought about it. Thought about it as she drove home—yes, she'd begun to think of her grandmother's house as home—and she thought about it as she finished the attic. She thought about it, dreamed about it, fantasized about it…

Ironically enough, in the pictures that chronicled her grandma's life, she saw plenty of evidence that her grandma had known how to relax, and be wild and free.

How was it her grandmother had never insisted on getting to see her only grandchild?

It made her sad. It made her feel alone. She had missed out on something, something she needed badly.

Affection.

A sense of belonging.

Love.

Damn, enough with the self-pity. Having finished the attic, she moved down a floor to box up her grandmother's bedroom. There she made an even bigger find than pictures—her grandmother's diaries. Brooke stared down at one dated ten years back, the year she'd graduated from high school.

I tried calling my daughter today but she's changed her number. Probably long gone again on another of her moves. Of course she didn't think to let me know the new number, or where she's going.

She's still mad at me.

I really thought I was doing the right thing, telling her what I thought of her bohemian lifestyle and the shocking way she drags that child across the world for her own pleasure. I thought she needed to hear my opinion.

For years I thought that.

Now I know different. I know it's her life to live as she wants, and if I'd only arrived at this wisdom sooner, I wouldn't be alone now, with no one to belong to and no one to belong to me.

Brooke remembered that year. Her mother had gone after some guy to Alaska, and she'd entered junior college in Florida, feeling extremely…alone. Hugging the diary to her chest, she stared blindly out the window, wondering how different her life might have been if stubbornness hadn't been the number one trait in her grandmother's personality…

Or her mother's.

Or hers…

IF ANYONE had asked, Zach would have said he spent his days off surfing with Eddie and Sam, and replacing the brakes and transmission on his truck.

What he wouldn't have mentioned was how much time he spent thinking about Brooke. They most definitely had some sort of an attraction going on, one he wanted to explore. He wished she'd taken him up on spending some of their days off together. His weekend might have turned out differently if she had.

But with too much time to think, he'd gone over and over the Hill Street fire, the one he was so sure had been arson.

Tommy wouldn't give him any info. He and Tommy went way back to when Tommy had sat on the hiring board that had plucked Zach out of the academy, but the inspector wasn't playing favorites. Sharp as hell and a first-rate investigator, he was as overworked as the rest of them and frustrated at Zach's pressing the issue. All week his response had remained the same: "I'm working on it."

Still, Zach found himself driving to the site, where he'd gotten an unhappy shock. Back on the night of the fire he'd only had three minutes before the chief had ordered everyone out, just long enough for him to catch sight of *two* points of origin. One in the kitchen beneath the sink, the other in the kid's bedroom inside a wire-mesh trash can.

But now the kid's bedroom had been cleaned, and there was no sight of the wire-mesh trash can or flash point marring the wall.

And no sign of an ongoing fire investigation.

What *didn't* shock Zach was finding Tommy waiting for him at the start of his next shift.

Tommy was a five-foot-three Latin man with a God complex compounded by short-man syndrome. Added to this, ever since his doctor had made him give up caffeine, he'd been wearing a permanent surly frown; now was no exception as he stalked up to Zach as he got out of his truck. "We need to talk."

Zach shut his door without locking it. No one ever locked their doors in Santa Rey. "Still off caffeine, huh?"

"The Hill Street fire."

Zach sighed. "What about it?"

"I just left the scene."

"Okay." Zach nodded and grabbed his gear bag out of the back of his truck. "So maybe you can tell me what happened to the second point of origin, the one I saw in the kid's bedroom the night of the fire."

Tommy's jaw bunched. "The fire is out. Your job is done."

Zach turned to look at him, and it was Tommy's turn to sigh. "We found the point of origin in the kitchen. Beneath the sink. There were rags near the cleaning chemicals, which ignited. The fire alarm was faulty and didn't go off. It wasn't called in by anyone in the house, but by an anonymous tip reporting smoke."

"There was a metal trash can in the kid's room—"

"Zach, stop." Tommy's voice was quiet but his eyes were intense. "The chief's signing off on the report today. Accidental ignition."

"He can't sign off. It's arson."

"I'm not having this conversation." Tommy turned and started to walk away. "Not with you."

"Are you kidding me?"

Tommy looked back, regret creeping into his expression. "Look, you're not the most credible of witnesses right now, okay? There were those two other fires earlier in the season that you cried arson—"

"*Cried arson?* What am I, the boy who cried wolf?"

"Just leave the case to those who are trained, Zach. I've got a helluva workload right now and I don't need you—"

"I don't care about your workload. We're *all* over-worked. What I care about is making sure that whoever killed that kid pays his due."

"*My* job, Zach. My job."

"But you don't believe it was arson."

Tommy gave him one hard, long stare. "I never said that."

"What the hell does that mean?"

"Look, I get that after what happened to your parents, that you'd see arson in every fire, but—"

No. Oh, hell, no. "We dealt with that in my interview, remember? That fire was years ago and has nothing to do with this."

"Are you saying that what happened to them when you were a kid has nothing to do with you being a fire-fighter?"

"I'm saying that I know what I saw on that Hill Street fire."

"No, you don't." Tommy scrubbed a weary hand over his face. "Listen, you should have several strikes on your permanent record by now, but I've always stepped in for you. I trusted you, and now I'm asking you to trust me."

"To do what?"

"To not go over my head with this. The chief is getting pissed off, Zach. And when he's pissed, he reacts. You know that by now. So do this, for me." He paused. *"Please."* And with that, he walked away.

Zach watched him leave in frustrated disbelief before turning to go inside, coming face-to-face with Brooke.

"Hey," she said softly.

"Hey." Before he could ask how much she'd over-heard, she put her hand on his arm and literally gave him a physical jolt. Gave her one, too, by the way she pulled her hand back. Jesus, when they finally touched each other sexually—and they would—he was convinced they'd spontaneously combust.

"You okay?"

Better now, he thought. "Yeah." He took her hand in his, and felt the jolt all the way to his toes. "Quite a zap."

"Yeah."

Something about her made him forget his troubles. Well, not forget, but be able to ignore them, anyway. Her eyes were soft and also somehow sweet. After nearly three weeks, Number Seven had finally let her guard down, and damn, but it looked good on her. He wondered if she wanted to put that concern to good use, because he had several ideas—

"Are you sure you're okay?"

Soft, sweet, sexy, and too perceptive. "I'm fine."

"Because it's understandable if you're not. I'm here if you wanted to—"

Oh yeah. He wanted to. He wanted to in his bed, in hers, with her panting out his name as she came all over him.

"—talk."

He blinked the sexy vision away. "No. Not talk."

She blushed but didn't go there. "I'm sorry about your parents."

So she'd heard everything. "It was a long time ago."

"And it doesn't change what you saw at that Hill Street fire."

He stared at her, a little stunned. "No, it doesn't." He felt his heart engage, hard. "You're different, Brooke O'Brien."

"I've heard that before."

"Different good. Different great."

She didn't believe him, that was all over her face. "If you'd gone surfing with me," he said, "I could have shown you, proven it to you."

"Maybe another time."

Now that, he could get behind. "I'll count on it."

With an unsure but endearing nod, she walked away.

5

IF BROOKE HAD TALKED with Zach for even another minute, she'd probably have thrown herself at him. She wouldn't have been able to help herself. He'd been standing there, looking fiercely unhappy, and her ears had been ringing with all she'd heard Tommy say to him—about his parents, about that kid dying, about how Zach needed to stay out of it. God, she'd wanted to grab him and hug him and kiss away that look on his face.

Even now she wanted to, hours later, sitting by herself in the house.

Good thing she was off duty for two days. Two days in which to get herself together and find some semblance of control. Because there were other ways to offer comfort than sex, for God's sake. She could buy a Hallmark card, for instance. Or make cookies.

But neither appealed. No, she wanted to offer a different kind of comfort all together.

A physical comfort.

A grip. She needed one. So she buried herself in packing. By the time her weekend was over, she'd gotten to the halfway point, setting aside a shocking amount of boxes to keep.

Keep.

Odd, how she wished she could keep even more, but she'd talked herself out of that, going only for the photos and diaries, still surprised at the sentimental impulse. What was she going to do with it all and no house to keep it in? Oh sure, her name was on the deed of this one, but that was temporary.

Like everything in her life.

The answers didn't come, not then, and not when she drove to work for her next scheduled shift. As she got out of her car, her eyes automatically strayed to the hammock, empty of one übersexy firefighter. Not there.

And not washing his rig, half-naked. His rig was parked, though, so she knew he was here, somewhere. Pulse quickening for no good reason other than she was thinking about him, she stepped inside her new home away from home and found a big poster had gone up in the front room, announcing the chief's upcoming big birthday beach bash.

A party.

She wasn't great at those. Turning to head into the kitchen, she ran smack into a warm, solid chest.

Zach's T-shirt didn't say Bite Me today. It didn't say anything. No, this one was plain black, half-tucked into loosely fitted Levi's that looked like beloved old friends, faded in all the stress points. He had his firefighter duffel bag over his shoulder and was clearly just getting here for his shift, same as her.

"Hey." It was the low, rough voice that had thrilled her in waaaay too many of her dreams lately. "You showed."

At the old refrain said after all these weeks only to make her smile, she found herself doing just that even as her body came to quick, searing life. She had it bad for him, and it was as hot and uncontrollable as a flash fire. "I told you, I finish everything I start."

He smiled a bad-boy smile, and touched her, a hand to hers, that was all—and the whole of her melted. "Everything?" he murmured.

Oh, boy. She recognized the heat in his gaze, and felt a matching heat in her belly.

And her nipples.

And between her legs.

A kiss. She wanted just one kiss. Was that so bad?

"Because I think we've started something very interesting here. Something we should finish. What do you think?"

"I…uh…"

"I'm all ears," he murmured and shifted just a little closer. So close that she had to tip her head up to see into his eyes, giving her an up-front and personal view of the scar that slashed his right eyebrow in half.

Her gaze dropped from that scarred brow to his mouth. *Way* too dangerous. Also too sexy-looking for his own good, for *hers*—his smile too easy on the eyes, his *everything* too easy on the eyes.

"Brooke?"

"Don't I hear a fire bell?" she managed.

He chuckled softly. "No, but nice try." He shifted to let her move past him, but somehow they ended up bumping against each other, softness to hardness. For a brief breath she closed her eyes and allowed herself to absorb it—his scent, his proximity, the feel of him brushing up against her.

She'd had no idea how much she'd craved this nearness, a physical touch; that it was *him,* the object of her secret nighttime fantasies, only intensified the sensation.

He put his hands on her arms, sensuously slid them up and down, and she forgot they were in the firehouse, forgot that they should really make at least an attempt to be discreet. Hell, she forgot to breathe. "Zach." She tore her gaze from his and looked at his mouth.

A mouth that let out a low, rough sound of hunger, and then, blessedly, *finally,* was on hers, and then she was kissing him with *her* mouth, with her entire body, and most likely her heart and soul, because, good Lord, the man could kiss. He gave her everything—his hands, his body, his tongue—and when they broke apart for air, he stared down at her in astonishment. "Damn."

"What?"

"Just damn." Eyes a little dazed, he took a step back, looking off his axis enough to send a surge of lust and power skittering through her, but she managed to control herself. Controlled and composed. Yeah, that was her, one hundred percent put together.

With hard nipples.

And a telling dampness between her thighs.

"You ever feel anything like that before?" he asked.

"Truthfully? It's been so long, I can't remember."

His soft but not necessarily amused laugh ruffled the hair at her temple and ran down her spine. "Love your honesty."

She didn't. And she didn't love the idea that anyone could have seen that wild kiss they'd just shared. What was the matter with her? She turned away, but he caught her, a hand curving around her shoulder. "Don't go."

She needed to. *So* needed to. "Listen, maybe we could forget about this, at least until I figure out what it is."

His hand slid down her arm, settling on her waist,

where his thumb lazily stroked one of her ribs. The motion liquefied her bones and altered her breath. "Forget it? I don't think that's possible. Did you feel that?"

"I felt…something." Which she was fighting. She wasn't sure why, when she'd wanted that kiss more than her next breath—but that hadn't been just any kiss. No. And being with him wouldn't be just sex, either, and she knew herself enough to know that she wasn't quite equipped to walk away. Not from that.

And she *was* walking away. In a matter of weeks. Her job would be over, her grandmother's home on the market… "It's natural that we'd feel…" She watched him arch a curious brow. "This. Natural. I'm a woman, you're a man." A really, *really* hot man, but still. "Natural," she repeated again, and tried to mean it. "We've been working hard, and not relaxing, and…"

His head dipped to hers, his eyes a lethal combo of heat and good humor. "So you'd feel this with everyone, then? Say, Dustin? Or Blake?"

"Okay, no. But—"

Triumph surged in his eyes to go with that heart-stopping heat. "Maybe we should do something about it."

Yes, cried her body. Oh please, yes.

A bell sounded, thank God, and before she could form a response, the call went out for all the firefighters, no EMTs required.

Aidan popped his head in for Zach, who nodded, then looked down into her face. "We can finish this when I get back."

"No need," she said quickly.

"Oh, there's a need."

And then he was gone.

BROOKE SPENT most of the day out on transport calls with Dustin, and though she gave her all to what she was doing, her mind wandered. Not to the house she needed to sell, or how it was going to make her feel to leave a place she was slowly, reluctantly, started to think of as hers, but to a man and his kiss, and to the fact that he was making her yearn and burn when she never yearned and burned.

"Where are you today, New Hire? Disneyland?" Dustin shot her an exasperated look after having to ask her the same question three times in a row.

"I'm sorry. I'm preoccupied."

He pushed up his glasses. "It's because you guys haven't knocked it out yet. That's very preoccupying."

She stared at him. *"What?"*

"Come on. Are you going to tell me that you don't want to be with Zach?"

"Yes," she said quickly. "I'm going to tell you that. I don't want to be with…"

He waited patiently, but the lie wouldn't come off her damn tongue. Frustrated, she turned to look out the window, watching the town go by. Farmers' market. An art gallery. An outdoor café. "It's personal."

"Hey, don't worry. Your secret's safe with me. Hell, I've got the same problem."

"You want to have sex with Zach?"

He pushed up his glasses again, grinned, and pulled into the station. "Not quite." He hopped out and walked away whistling, getting inside before she could ask him *who* he had the same problem with.

Zach and Aidan's rig was in the garage, and her heart skipped a beat. The kiss, the kiss, the kiss…it was all she could think about. That, and getting another. And then she stepped into the kitchen and found Zach just standing there, looking ten kinds of wow.

He was in his gear, a little dusty, a little sooty and a whole lot sexy. He was still practically shimmering with adrenaline from the fire he'd just fought, looking far too edgy to be the laid-back, easygoing surfer guy she knew him to be.

And far too much for her to handle, no matter how much her body sent up a plea to let it do just that. He was too experienced for her, too…everything.

She'd spent too much time in her life trying to get somewhere, trying to find herself, to let a man like this in. Unfortunately, right now, at this very second, she wasn't thinking about finding herself. She was thinking about seeing him naked. "Hey. You okay?"

"Yeah."

But that was a lie, and that haze of lust he always created faded a little as she stepped closer. "Did anyone get hurt?" Or God forbid, like in the Hill Street fire that she knew haunted him, die.

"No."

But the memory of something bad was etched in the drawn, exhausted lines of his face. He took his losses hard, very hard, and that fact only deepened how she felt about him.

"I'm just tired," he said. "And needed a moment alone."

"Oh. I'm sorry." And she went to leave, because she understood that, but then he added, "I don't want to be alone from you."

She turned to look at him, but he'd moved closer and

she bumped right into him. Her chest to his, his thighs to hers, and she actually let out a shuddering sigh that might have been a moan.

"What was that?"

Oh, just her brain cells blowing fuses left and right. "Nothing."

Snagging her hand, he held her close, peering into her face. "You let out a…sound."

"Yes. It's called breathing."

His hand slid to her waist and gently squeezed. "It sounded like more."

How about a sexually charged, needy whimper? Did it sound like that? "No."

His gaze searched hers for a moment. "Maybe we should talk about the kiss."

Kisses. Plural. "Probably we shouldn't. It might lead to…"

More.

He was waiting for her to speak.

"I think I heard the fire alarm."

"Huh," he said, sounding curious.

"What?"

"You're not as honest as I thought."

"Yes, I am."

"Really?" His hand slid to the small of her back and stroked lightly. "Then what are you thinking right now?"

That he'd look mighty fine naked. "That I'm hungry."

Not a lie. She *was* hungry. For his yummy body.

"Brooke…"

"Yeah. Listen." She let out a breath. "I'm trying to resist you here, okay? I'm failing miserably, but I'm trying."

"Why?"

Wasn't that the question of the year. "Because this is unlike me, this thing we have going on. I don't flirt, and I certainly don't do…whatever it is *you're* thinking right now."

"Never?"

"No, not—not in a long time."

"That's just not right, Brooke."

Just the image of what they were talking about gave her an odd shiver and changed her breathing, and she realized he wasn't breathing all that steadily, either. "Not helping, Zach."

He laughed—at himself, at her, she had no idea really, but she found herself staring up at him, torn between marveling at the ease with which he showed his emotions and laughing back because the sound of his genuine amusement was contagious. "Happy to amuse you."

"I'm sorry." Still smiling, he sighed. "Ah, hell, that felt good. Laughing."

"Laughing at me felt good."

"Oh, no." Gently, he tugged on her ponytail. "Definitely laughing with you, I promise. And I should be resisting, too. But I can't seem to do that."

His words caused more of those interesting shivers down her spine, and to other places, as well, secret places that wanted reactivating. Standing there in the hallway, way too close to this sexy man, a smile wanting to split her face, laughter spilling in her gut, she realized something.

Whether she'd meant to or not, she'd made roots here, temporary ones, but roots she would treasure and remember always. And now she wanted to strip naked and let him do things to her, lots of things, things that would create more lasting memories that she could take with her. "So how often, when you give that look to a woman, when you talk to her in that low, sexy voice, when you touch her, do her clothes just fall off?"

When he opened his mouth, she shook her head. "No, you know what? I'm sorry. Don't answer that. Because I was on board for that. The clothes-falling-off thing. But..."

"But...?"

"But I'm not mixing business and pleasure, no matter how sexy you are. I can't, much as I want to. I just can't, not for anything less than a meaningful, lasting relationship, a real connection."

Her own words shocked her but she found she meant them. To the bone. Being in her grandmother's house had obviously sent that yearning within her rising to the surface, and she couldn't help it. "I mean it. I'm sorry if I let you think otherwise, but I really do."

Looking torn between bafflement and disappointment, he nodded. "Okay."

"I'm sorry if I led you on. If it helps, I led myself on, too. I hope we're still friends." All that was left to do was walk away gracefully, when in her heart of hearts she didn't want to walk away at all. She started with one step, a baby step, and then another. "I also hope that the rest of your shift goes well," she managed.

"Thank you. That's...friendly of you."

Was he was mocking her? "Well," she said primly, backing to the door. "Just because we're not going to..."

"Mix business and pleasure," he supplied helpfully.

"Yes." Because obviously he was not looking for a deep or meaningful relationship, or he'd have said so. "It doesn't mean that we can't get along."

"I think," he said slowly, in a tone she couldn't quite place, "that we're not going to have a problem in that department."

No. No, they weren't.

She nodded, and managed to turn and leave, but in the hallway, alone, she leaned back against a wall and let out a long breath. There. That hadn't been hard or awkward.

Ah, hell. It'd been plenty of both.

But she'd done the right thing. Now she wouldn't fall for him and mourn him after she left. Yep, definitely the right thing.

Damn it. Why couldn't she have gotten all self-protective after she'd gotten to see him naked? Brooke turned around to look at the closed kitchen door, nearly going back in, but she restrained herself.

The right thing.

6

SEVERAL SHIFTS LATER, Brooke was sitting outside the fire station on a rare break, laptop open, flipping through a national job database to see where she might go after the house sold and this job ended in a few weeks.

The warm sun beat down on her, the waves across the street providing the perfect white noise. It should have been incredibly peaceful. Instead, she was thinking about Zach. About the kissing. About her opening her mouth and saying that she wasn't going to mix pleasure and business.

She'd meant it, but she *really* regretted saying it.

Cristina came outside. She wore her blue uniform trousers, a pair of kick-ass boots and a tiny white tank top, which emphasized a figure that a Playboy model would envy. Chomping into a red apple, she glanced at Brooke. "Are you actually relaxing, New Hire?"

"Brooke. My name's Brooke." This was now a three-week-old refrain between the two of them.

Hard to believe she'd been in California for so long already, but it was a fact. And as she always did, Cristina shrugged. "Hey, I called Number Four Skid Mark, so consider yourself lucky."

She would. Cristina might be sarcastic and caustic but

she was brutally honest, emphasis on brutally, and loyal to a fault. In short, if you were on her good side, you had a friend to the death. Brooke knew the two of them weren't there, not even close, but at least she didn't have a nickname she couldn't live with.

"There's no point in remembering your name when you all eventually quit," Cristina continued.

"I'm not leaving until my six weeks are up. I'm just past halfway."

Leaning back against a tree, Cristina studied Brooke with interest. "People who aren't from around here rarely stick."

"Gee, really? Even with your sweet and welcoming attitude?"

Cristina smiled. "It's too bad you're not sticking. You could grow on me."

"I *am* sticking. Until the job is over."

"Speaking of sticking, I hear you were sticking to Officer Hottie's lips. That true?"

Oh, boy. "Officer Hottie?"

"Yeah. So were you?"

"That's…" She settled for the same line she'd given Dustin. "Personal."

"How personal?"

Wasn't that the question. She and Zach had only kissed, but it seemed like more, and there'd been lots of close encounters since… All she knew was that the wild sexual tension seemed unrelenting.

And overwhelming.

She really wanted to face that tension, and release it.

Let loose.

Assuming Zach still wanted to.

"I know my faults," Cristina said into her silence. "I'm sarcastic, mean and I don't like many people. But Zach? I like him. A whole lot. He's going through a tough time, and he's vulnerable."

The thought of big, rough-and-tumble Zach being vulnerable might have been funny only a week ago but Brooke knew Cristina was right. "The arson thing?"

"The chief's riding Tommy's ass, and Tommy's riding Zach's. Zach could just shut up and walk away from it all, but it's not in his blood to walk away, not when he knows he's right. I care about him, we all care about him, and he needs to stay focused."

"How do I threaten that?"

"You're messing with his head. *I'm* the only one who does that."

As warnings went, it wasn't exactly subtle. "I didn't realize you two were dating."

"Oh, I wouldn't call it dating," Cristina said with a smile.

Okaaaaay. "What would you call it?"

Cristina just looked smug, then, standing up, grabbed hold of a tree branch above her. "Any new interesting calls lately?"

"Hard to top Viagra Man, but I'm sure there's something just around the corner. What are you doing?"

"Pull-ups." She did five in a row, and still managed to talk normally. "Cats and hard-ons. Interesting job, you have to admit."

"True."

"So where are you going when this is over?"

"Don't worry. It'll be far, far away." Brooke just wished she knew where. She always knew—but this time nothing was coming to her.

Looking pleased, Cristina executed ten more pull-ups, then dropped to the ground to do push-ups.

Brooke went back to her laptop. Cristina didn't seem to mind being ignored, and Brooke tried for some peace and quiet. When another set of footsteps came up the walk, she didn't even bother to look up. She was busy, very busy, thank you very much, and needed no more distractions.

"Didn't anyone ever tell you that all work and no play will make you a very dull girl?"

Everything within her went still at the sound of Zach's low, husky voice. He wore his uniform, looking just hot enough that she felt little flickers of flame burst to life inside her. "Maybe I like dull."

"Nobody likes dull."

"I don't know." This from Cristina, now doing sit-ups on the grass like a machine. "I can believe she likes dull."

With an irritated sigh, Brooke closed her laptop yet again and stood. She'd find another place to study. Some place where the not-so-subtle barbs couldn't pierce her skin. Some place where there were no gorgeous, sexy firefighters making her yearn for things she shouldn't, like a connection, a real connection. And letting loose… She made it to the door before a big, warm hand hooked her elbow and pulled her around.

For a guy who only moved when he needed to, she was surprised at how fast he'd caught her. "I'm busy," she said with unmistakable irritation. She used that tone when she needed someone to back off, and it'd never failed her.

But it failed her now. Utterly.

"Yes, I can see that you're very busy."

Cristina, apparently finished torturing her body, walked past them with a smirk.

But Zach just studied Brooke's face. "You're always busy. You like it that way."

So damn true. But they weren't going there. "Where were you?"

"A meeting with the chief."

He was no longer amused, and she read between the lines. "How did it go?"

"Terrific."

"Really?"

"Sure. All I have to do is learn to respect authority, and everything will be just terrific. So were you and Cristina bonding?"

Nice subject change, she thought, but she saw misery in his eyes, and she didn't want to poke at it. "Yeah. We're like this." She held up two entwined fingers.

He smiled.

"Officer Hottie?" she asked. "Really?"

He had the good grace to wince. "If it helps, I don't answer to it." It was just the two of them in the yard now, with no company except the light breeze and waves. Perfect time to tell him she wanted to mix business and pleasure, just once. He stood close enough that she could see flecks of dark jade swimming in that sea of pale green. He hadn't shaved this morning, and maybe not yesterday morning, either, and she could feel the heat radiating off his body and seeping into hers. She could smell him, too, some delicious, intoxicating scent of pure male that had her nostrils twitching.

Bad nostrils. *Tell him...*

"Cristina doesn't mean to be rude," Zach said.

It made her laugh. "Yes, she does."

"Okay, yeah. She does."

"You're all a very tight unit. I get that loud and clear."

"We are. It's what makes us so good. But there's room for more. There's room for you. You could fit in, if you wanted to."

Her greatest fantasy… "*If* I wanted to?"

"Yeah, well, you have a tendency to stand on the outside looking in."

"No, I don't."

He just looked at her, all patient and quietly amused, and she sighed. "Okay, I do."

"But you don't want to be on the outside looking in."

How was it that he knew her? "We both know I don't really fit in."

"You could."

"Uh-huh. Cristina's waiting with open arms."

His expression was serious now. "She's had it rough and is a little distrustful, that's all. It has nothing to do with you."

She had a feeling it wasn't only Cristina who'd had it rough. "You're sleeping with her."

Brooke hadn't meant for that to escape from her lips. She wanted to pretend it hadn't, but Zach's brows had shot up so far on his forehead they vanished into his hair.

"Not that it matters," she said quickly, trying like hell to backtrack. "Because it doesn't."

"It doesn't?"

She shook her head. "It doesn't. It really doesn't. It really, really, *really* doesn't—"

He set a finger on her lips and she shut up.

"Cristina and I are friends," he said quietly. "We have been for a very long time."

She wrapped her fingers around his wrist and pulled it away. "And more than friends? Have you been more than friends for a very long time, as well?"

"Twice. A very long time ago."

She didn't want to acknowledge the relief that flooded through her at that. "You might want to remind her of that part the next time she's going around marking her territory."

"She has no territory to mark. Or I never would have kissed you like I did." He ran a finger over her jaw.

A simple touch.

But there was nothing simple about the way her body reacted, starting with the breath backing up in her throat and her nipples tightening as they hoped for some attention, too. So much for not mixing business and pleasure, because there was pleasure when she was with him. Lots of it. "Oh boy."

His gaze met hers. "Oh boy bad, or oh boy good?"

"We're friends."

"Yes."

"Th-that touch felt like…more."

"Did it?" He smiled innocently. "Then *you're* the one mixing the business with the pleasure, aren't you?"

She stared at him, but he only smiled, touched her again, then walked off, leaving her to talk to herself. "Am not," she whispered.

But she was.

She *so* was.

THE NEXT DAY, Brooke and Dustin hit the ground running and never slowed. They delivered a baby at a grocery store, transported a set of conjoined twins, stood by at a bank robbery and helped locate two fingers belonging to a construction worker, who'd lost them in a pile of sawdust thanks to the blade of his handsaw. It was early evening before they finally made their way back to the station, where a delicious smell had Brooke's nose twitching.

"Ohmigod," Dustin moaned. "Smell that?"

"Tell me it's for us."

"If there's a God."

Following the scent into the kitchen, they found the crew grabbing plates and helping themselves to a huge pan of lasagna. Zach was already seated at the table, his uniform trousers and a gray T-shirt spread taut over that hard body.

Brooke's gaze locked on his. They hadn't spoken since yesterday, where she'd done that whole mixing-business-with-pleasure thing, confusing their issues.

Her issues.

The memory of their kiss—that deep, hot long kiss—was *still* burned in her mind. In spite of herself, she wanted another one, and she had a feeling it was all over her face.

"Ah, man," Aidan moaned loudly from the table, mouth full—which didn't stop him from loading more in. "This lasagna is better than sex."

Cristina snorted. "Then you're doing it wrong." She took a bite, then also moaned. "But, oh yeah, baby, this is a close second. Nicely done, Officer Hottie."

Zach rolled his eyes. "Thanks. I think."

Brooke stared at him as she sat. "You cooked?"

"Well, we tried letting Cristina cook," Aidan said. "Remember, Eeyore?" He nudged Blake with his elbow. "For your birthday?"

"Disaster," Blake confirmed with a dour nod.

Aidan nodded, winking at Brooke as he successfully ruffled Cristina's feathers. "Cristina here burns water with spectacular flare."

"Hey, I've got other talents," Cristina said.

Aidan grinned. "Sure you do."

Cristina waved her fork in his face. "Don't make me kick your ass."

"You cooked," Brooke repeated, looking at Zach.

"Why are you so surprised?"

"Because—" Because it was a hidden talent, and now she was wondering at his other hidden talents. "I'm just impressed, that's all."

"Well, welcome to the twenty-first century," Cristina muttered, still glaring at Aidan. "Where men cook. And in case you haven't heard, us women can vote now, too."

Everyone laughed, and Brooke rolled her eyes, but when she looked around, she realized they weren't laughing *at* her at all. She was included in the joke.

Zach was gazing at her, his mouth curved, looking relaxed and easygoing and, damn it, gorgeous, and something came to her in that moment.

She belonged.

Aidan and Cristina were still bickering, Blake and Dustin were thumb wrestling for the last serving of lasagna, Sam and Eddie were shoveling in their food and laughing over something…they were all as dysfunctional as they could be, and they were a family.

And she was a part of it.

Sam took the last of the lasagna and everyone protested. "Hey, there's two kinds of people in here—the fast and the hungry. I'm the fast, that's all."

Zach smiled at Brooke with a genuine affection that stole her breath.

And replaced it with heat.

Oh boy, a lot of heat.

"Hey," Sam said. "Don't forget, I need everyone to sign up for party duty. The chief's b-day bash isn't going to throw itself."

"Yeah, and why are we doing this again?" Blake asked, classic Eeyore.

"To have an excuse to have a party," Eddie explained.

"To kiss up, you mean," Blake said, sounding disgusted with all of them. "Don't forget the kissing-up part."

"Well, maybe if Zach spent some time kissing up—" Sam accompanied this with kiss-kiss noises "—he wouldn't be called to the principal's office to get spanked every other day."

Zach sighed.

Cristina reached across the table and squeezed his hand. "I'd rather be spanked than hold my tongue."

"Me, too," Aidan said, in between mouthfuls of food. "Me, too."

"Yes, but…" Blake sent Zach a frustrated look. "It wouldn't hurt to lay low, let the chief get distracted by someone else's ass once in a while."

Zach shook his head.

No can do on the lying low thing, apparently.

"I can tell on Sam," Eddie suggested. "For leaving porn in the bathroom. Maybe that would take some of the heat off Zach."

"Hey, what did porn ever do to you?" Sam protested.

They all laughed, and Zach smiled, but Brooke could see that it didn't reach his eyes.

Later, she sought him out in the kitchen. He opened the refrigerator for a bottle of water, then leaned back against the counter, taking a long drink. He was behaving himself. Not mixing business and pleasure.

He was also quiet. Hurting.

Telling herself she was crazy, she walked toward him and took the water from his hand.

He just looked at her.

"That friend thing…" she started.

"Yeah?" He gripped the edges of the counter by his sides, and she wondered if that was to ensure he didn't touch her. She wished he could have put those hands on her, but she'd seen to it that he wouldn't try.

For her own good.

Damn, she was tired of for her own good. "If we're friends," she said softly, "then I should be able to do this."

"What?"

She set her hands on his chest, then let them glide up around his neck, bringing her body flush to his as she hugged him.

For one beat he held himself rigid, then with a low, rough breath, let his hands drop from the counter and come around her, hard.

She didn't look into his face, knowing if she did, she'd kiss him again, and this was just a hug, comfort.

Friendship.

So she pressed her face into his throat and held on.

"Brooke," he murmured, and the hand he had fisted in her shirt low on her back opened, pressing her even closer as he buried his face in her hair and just breathed her in. "Brooke—"

The kitchen door opened, and Eddie looked at them, brows raised. "If I cook tomorrow," he asked, "can I have the same thank-you?"

MUCH LATER THAT NIGHT, back at her grandmother's house, Brooke thought about the evening. About the hug and her reaction to it. Partially, because her body was still revved from what should have been an innocent touch, but there was more to it.

According to Sam, she could be the fast, or the hungry. But when it came to her life, she'd always been the fast, never slowing down, never relaxing, always doing, going, running. And for what? To always end up alone, wondering what she was missing? She'd come here out of duty, but she'd also wanted to find herself. Maybe…maybe she couldn't do that at the speed of light, maybe she had to slow down. Maybe *that's* what was missing.

She needed to give herself time to catch her breath, time to relax.

Needed to do that whole let-loose thing.

Moving through the kitchen with a mug of tea, she looked out the window at the dark night and thought about it, thought about Zach. As she did, a now-familiar tingle began low in her belly and spread. And suddenly, she had a feeling she knew exactly how she should be letting loose. And it included mixing business and pleasure.

A *lot* of mixing.

7

ZACH RAN in the mornings. It woke him up, kept him in shape and gave him time to think. Typically, he thought about work or, more recently, Brooke. He really liked thinking about Brooke.

But this morning, after having a dream about the arson fire, it wasn't Brooke on his mind, and he changed his routine, running past Hill Street. When he reached the fire site, he thought maybe he was still dreaming.

The place had been demolished, razed.

He stared at it in disbelief. On a hunch, he ran back to his house, got into his truck and drove to the site of a different fire, the one from a few months previous, a fire he'd also "cried" arson to Tommy about and had gotten his wrist slapped for.

That property was also demolished.

And the one before that? Yeah. Demolished. Standing at the edge of the third lot, where nothing remained but dirt, he pulled out his cell phone, but didn't hit any numbers as his last meeting with the chief ran through his head. He'd been asked, and not very nicely, to do his own job and no one else's.

Somehow he doubted stalking the fire sites would be considered doing his own job.

Shit.

Tommy Ramirez had told him to be on his best behavior, but that was proving damn hard to do. Driving home, he called Aidan, but had to leave a message. While waiting for a return call, he tried to distract himself with a Lakers game but his mind kept wandering to the arson.

He couldn't let it go. Driven to do something, Zach pulled out his laptop. He'd already typed up all his thoughts and notes on the fires. Now he needed to talk it out with someone, and oddly enough, the person that kept coming to mind wasn't Aidan, but someone with sweet baby blues and a smile that pretty much destroyed him.

Brooke. He was driven by her, too, because, damn, she was something. She was something, and…and she wanted a relationship.

Driven as he was, he didn't do relationships. Relationships always came to an end, and he hated endings. He didn't need a shrink to attribute that to losing his parents so young, to growing apart from the brother he had nothing in common with except grief and, in a way, losing him, too.

No, he didn't like endings, and therefore, avoided beginnings.

Still, Brooke drew him. She was a little buttoned-up, a little rigid, and—and hell. She had a smile that could melt him from across town, and a way of looking at him that suggested she could see right through to all his flaws, and she didn't mind those flaws.

Jesus. He went back to his laptop, burying himself. He had property deeds, architectural plans, records of sales, and looked it all over for the hundredth time to see if there were any obvious connections.

When his doorbell rang, he figured it was Aidan. When he opened the door, it turned out to be a beautiful redhead.

Nope, not Aidan, but his neighbor Jenny with a pizza in one hand, a six-pack dangling from her other, and a fuck-me smile firmly in place.

"Hi, neighbor." She lifted the pizza. "Interested?"

She was a high school librarian, but nothing about her was a stereotypical keeper of books. She hosted a weekly poker party, enjoyed car racing, and brewed her own beer. They were friends, and so far, *just* friends, but she'd made it clear that she was ready for that to change. Now here she was, flirting. Normally he'd flirt right back, but he didn't. Stress, he decided. Stress and frustration. "I'm sorry, Jenny. It's not a good time—"

"Don't even try to tell me you're not hungry. I'll have to take your temperature." She pushed her way in, carrying the food, swinging the beer. "Everyone has to eat."

True. And she'd obviously decided the way to his heart was by way of his stomach, maybe with a side trip past other certain body parts. Up until a few weeks ago, he might have been happy to take that side trip, but he no longer wanted to. Not with another woman on his mind.

Jenny turned to face him, and her smile slowly faded. "What's the matter?"

"I'm not sure." Yes. Yes, he was. He wanted a blue-eyed, sweet, sexy EMT with a smile that slayed him.

And only her.

"Zach?" Jenny waved a hand in front of his face. "You look like you were just hit by a train."

Uh-huh. The Brooke train. At some point, probably during the wild kiss, he'd decided no one else would do. *Holy shit.*

Jenny set down the food and popped the top off two of the beers, handing him one. "Here. You look like you could use this now."

"Thanks." He took a long pull.

"So who is she?"

"I didn't even know there was a she until two seconds ago. How did you know?"

"It's all over your face."

He scrubbed a hand over his face, images of Brooke coming to him. That very first day when she'd woken him, or when she'd so fiercely approached Code Calico, and then Viagra Man…or the way she'd looked at him with her heart and soul in her eyes when she'd said she wanted a relationship.

"Damn," Jenny said softly, still staring at him. "She's…special, isn't she?"

"I—yeah." He managed to meet her gaze. "I'm sorry."

"Not as sorry as I am." With another sigh, she stepped toward him, and in a show of how stunned he was, managed to nudge him down to the couch with a single finger. Then she plopped next to him and clinked her bottle to his in a commiserating toast. "You're good and screwed, you know that, right?"

He leaned back and shook his head. "You have no idea."

ON THE DRIVE to work, Brooke took in the high morning surf on her left, and the joggers, walkers and bikers on her right. She'd lost track of how many times she'd moved in her life, but all of those places had been big cities. She had to admit small-town living appealed. Little to no traffic, good parking spots…

But she was almost four weeks down, and only two to

go. Past halfway. Soon enough she'd be gone, far away from here, starting over yet again. She'd found jobs available in both Seattle and L.A., and had filled out applications, telling herself there was just something about the West Coast.

But actually, there was just something about Santa Rey, and it had little to do with the great weather and everything to do with the fact that in spite of herself, she was making ties here.

Blake was on his laptop when she entered the firehouse, and at the sight of her, he jumped guiltily, quickly slapping the computer shut.

"Don't worry," she quipped. "Your porn is safe with me."

Instead of laughing, he grabbed his laptop and left the room.

Cristina was on one of the couches reading a *Cosmo*. She flipped a page. "Hey, New Hire. Maybe you should read this when I'm done. There's an article here on how not to scare off men."

Brooke shot her an exasperated look. "One of these days you're going to call me Brooke."

"I doubt it. Oh, and don't forget to read this article. 'How Not To Be Annoying At The Work Place.'"

Giving up, Brooke went into the kitchen. Her eyes automatically strayed to the counter—the scene of her two indiscretions: one a heart-stopping kiss, the other the best hug she'd ever had. Letting out a breath, she poured herself some iced tea and was adding sugar when the door opened behind her.

"Hey."

At just the one word, uttered in that easygoing, low,

husky voice, she dropped her spoon. "Damn it." She crouched down, and so did Zach, handing her the spoon, smiling at her. He was in uniform, filling it out with that mouthwatering body, but there was something...quiet about him today. Something quiet and, frankly, also outrageously sexy.

He helped her up. "You've been getting sun." He touched the tip of her nose. "And a few freckles." He stroked his finger over her cheek, her jaw.

Her body was so pathetically charged her toes curled at his touch. That's what happened when she spent her spare time dreaming about seeing him naked.

"You're looking at me funny again. Do I have something in my teeth?"

"No."

"Do I smell bad?"

That tugged a laugh out of her. He smelled delicious, and she suspected he knew it. "No."

"Then what?"

"I dreamed about you," she admitted.

"Ah. Were we mixing business and pleasure?"

She opened her mouth to say yes, oh most definitely yes, but then shut it again. No need to give him more power.

He just laughed softly. "We were, weren't we?"

She felt the blush creep up her cheeks.

"Yeah." Another low laugh and a naughty grin. "We were."

"Zach—"

"Was it good?"

She bit her lower lip but it must have been all over her face because his eyes went all sexy and sleepy. "Off the charts, huh?"

She closed her eyes. Oh yeah, off the charts.

Tell him you want to do the mixing in person. She was still trying to find the words when he said with a smile, "So, exactly how off the charts were we?"

"Zach!" yelled Dustin from the other room. "Phone!"

Zach sighed. "I'll be back. Don't move."

When he was gone, she let out a breath and fanned her face, saying the words she'd meant to say in front of him. "I was wrong. I *want* to mix business and pleasure. Just once." She smacked her own forehead. "How hard is *that* to say?"

Behind her, someone cleared his throat.

Oh, God. Wincing, she turned around. Blake had come in the back door in his silent way and stood there. "Sorry."

She just closed her eyes.

"No, it's okay. I didn't hear anything."

"Nothing?"

"Nothing," he said.

"Really?"

"Nothing except you want to jump his bones."

"I didn't say that!"

"Then I didn't hear it." He strode to the refrigerator, where he scrounged around and pulled out a soda, raising a brow when he realized she was still staring at him. "What? I won't tell anyone."

"Everyone tells everyone everything around here."

He acknowledged that with a shrug of his shoulders.

"Okay, you know what? I'm going to need a secret of yours."

He choked on his soda. "What?"

"That way I can guarantee that neither of us will talk."

Blake looked at her, then turned away. "I don't think that's a good idea."

"Are you kidding? It's a great idea."

His narrow shoulders were tense now. "But my secret is really someone else's."

"What do you mean?"

"Nothing. Never mind." Abruptly, he set his soda on the counter and walked out.

"Blake?"

But he was gone, carrying her very revealing secret. And then the fire bell went off and she put it out of her mind.

LATER THAT DAY, Brooke and Dustin were in the kitchen devouring a box of cookies between them while standing in front of the opened refrigerator trying to cool off.

"We're having a poker game Friday night at Cristina's," Dustin said. "You should join us."

"Did you ask Cristina?"

"Don't worry about her. She'll be happy to see you."

"Happy? Really? Cristina?"

"Okay," he said with a fond smile. "So she can be aloof, but it's just a facade. She's really just a toasted marshmallow."

"What did you call me?" Cristina came into the kitchen. She was in the bottom half of her fire gear, with a snug T-shirt on top. Her hair was pulled back and she looked hot, grumpy and irritated as she grabbed a handful of cookies.

"A *toasted* marshmallow." Dustin grinned at her, leaning back against the counter. "Crispy on the outside, soft and gushy on the inside."

Cristina hopped up on the counter next to him and set her head back against the upper cabinets, arms and legs spread in the aggressive sprawl of an alpha female who knew her place in the world. "Dustin?"

"Yeah?"

"The next time you call me a marshmallow, I'm going to pound you into the ground." She uttered this threat with her eyes closed, without moving a single muscle. "Next time."

Dustin winked at Brooke. "Definitely crispy on the outside."

"I can be a marshmallow sometimes, too," Brooke said.

A sound escaped Cristina, who still didn't move or open her eyes. "You don't know crispy. Dustin? Get me a water?"

"Ah, but I didn't hear the magic word."

"Get me a water. *Please.*"

"See?" Dustin grinned as he reached for a glass. "Soft and mushy."

"I'll have you know there's not a single inch of soft and mushy on me anywhere," Cristina muttered without her usual heat, making Brooke take a closer look at her. The female firefighter looked pale and just a little clammy, alerting her to the fact that maybe Cristina wasn't just being her usual pissy self, but might actually be in pain. "Hey, are you okay?"

"Migraine." Dustin filled the glass, which he gently nudged into Cristina's hands. Then he lay a cold, wet compress over her forehead.

"Thanks." Cristina let out a sigh. "Christ, this sucks. I'm going to the chief's party tonight. No matter what, I'm going."

"You should go home and sleep this off," Dustin said.

"I know. But first…" She sat up and groaned. "I've got to clean out my unit from that last call. Blake's doing something for the chief, so—"

Dustin set his hand to the middle of her chest and held her down. "If you're going to get rid of that headache, you need to sit real still and you know it."

The bell rang, and Cristina moaned, covering her ears as dispatch called for her and Blake's unit.

Dustin headed for the door. "I'll tell them you can't. They can get a different unit."

"Dustin—"

"Save it." He left the room.

Brooke looked at Cristina, so carefully still, pale and clearly miserable. "Can I get you anything?"

"Got a spare head?"

"Why don't you go home and go to bed?"

"I can't go anywhere until the rig is cleaned. We've got an inspection today."

"I know. We're all in the same boat."

"Oh, really? Are you on probation for falling asleep and not hearing a call?"

"Uh, no."

"Do you have a recent traffic violation?"

"Well, no, but—"

"Then get the hell out of my boat." Cristina sighed and straightened, looking positively green now. "Okay, I'm getting up. Watch your shoes."

"Stay." Brooke didn't quite dare put her hands on Cristina as Dustin had done, but she held them up. "I'll clean out your rig for you."

Cristina pulled the cold pack from her head and stared at Brooke. "Why? What do you want?"

Brooke let out a little laugh. "I'm offering to do something nice for you, even though you're not all that nice to me, and you're questioning it?"

"I'm less than 'not all that nice' to you, I'm downright bitchy. So the question stands, New Hire. Why would you do my job for me?"

Brooke shrugged. "Why not?"

Cristina just stared at her, the pain evident in her eyes but not hiding her cynicism. "The question isn't why not, but *why?*"

"Maybe I like to help people."

"We all do. Hence our jobs."

"Maybe I just do it nicer than you."

A ghost of a smile crossed Cristina's lips at that, then she very carefully covered her eyes with the compress again and leaned back. "Everyone does everything nicer than me."

"True," Dustin agreed, coming back into the room. "You're officially off duty, Cris."

Cristina peeked out from the cold pack to shoot him a look.

"You're sick. Take the break."

Cristina sighed. "Go away. Both of you just go away and let me die in peace."

Dustin lifted her off the counter.

"Hey!"

"If you won't put yourself to bed, I'll do it for you."

"Oh, sure, wait until I'm debilitated before you finally make a move on me."

He stared down at her, clearly shocked, his glasses slipping down his nose. "You want me to make a move on you?"

She didn't answer.

"Cristina?"

"There's a very real possibility I'm going to throw up on you. So if you could stop talking, that would help."

"And if you could stop trying to tell me what to do when you're as green as a leaf, that would help."

She laughed very very softly. "Assertive, too. Who knew? Hey, New Hire?"

Already heading for the door to go clean Cristina's rig, Brooke glanced over. "Yeah?"

"Thanks."

"A PARTY," Brooke muttered to herself. She'd showered and was now standing in the center of the bedroom she'd made hers, the first bedroom in her life that she loved without reason.

She had no idea if that was because her grandmother had put silly white-lace curtains over the window, which ruffled prettily in the wind, or if it was the dark cherry antique furniture. Or maybe it was because she'd come here looking for an exterior change of pace and had found an interior change of pace instead.

Because deep inside, she'd settled here. Her heart had engaged, for this town, this house.

For a man…

She stared into the closet. She had only one thing appropriate for a party on the beach, and that was a pretty little halter sundress she'd bought on a whim and had never worn.

With a sigh, she pulled it on, then didn't look at herself in the mirror. She did not want to change her mind. In that vein, she slipped into a pair of flip-flops and headed directly toward her car before she could come up with a million and one reasons not to go, starting with needing to work on the house and ending with because she was nervous.

Being nervous was not an option.

Not only was she going to go to this party, she was going to go and relax.

Let loose.

She needed to remember the concept. She needed to live the concept. She was going to smile and laugh. She was going to let go. And maybe even manage to do so with one wildly sexy Zach Thomas.

If he was still interested.

Please let him still be interested.

She drove to the beach, parked and got out of her car, the salty air brushing at her hair, the waves pounding the surf sounding all soft and romantic. Then she glanced over at the man getting out of the truck right next to her and her heart knocked hard into her ribs.

Zach wore board shorts and a T-shirt, his body looking at ease and beach ready. His eyes, though…not so relaxed. Nope. As she watched them lock on her, they were filled with the same hunger and frustration she felt, and she knew.

He was most definitely still interested.

8

IT HAD BEEN a shitty day all around, Zach thought as he got out of his truck. He'd had another unpleasant phone call with Tommy, who refused to tell him what was happening with the arsons. Then he'd covered for Cristina on three calls and as a result, hadn't been ready for their monthly inspection, and the chief had chewed him out.

Zach had almost not come tonight.

But now, looking into Brooke's eyes, he was suddenly glad he had. Very glad. Just taking her in, he felt a visceral reaction clear to his toes. For the first time since he'd met her, she wasn't dressed for the practicality of their work. No uniform trousers and matching shirt, no steel-toed work boots, no carefully controlled hairdo that said. *Back off. The rest of me is wound as tight as my hair.*

Not that *that* look didn't have some hotness to it.

But tonight she was in a pale blue sundress of some lightweight material that hugged toned limbs and a body that reminded him she was in shape.

Great shape.

She'd left her hair down, the strawberry blond strands falling in soft waves just past her shoulders, lit softly by the moonlight. A few long bangs were swept to one side, curving along her cheek and jaw, emphasizing her face.

A beautiful face.

Looking at him.

Smiling at him, with just a hint of nerves.

And he stood there, a little stunned, because when she smiled for real it lit up her face and her eyes, revealing humor and a sharp intelligence, and…and a sexual awareness that sparked his.

Hell, his had been sparked from the moment he'd first set eyes on her, but once he'd realized she wasn't going to play, he'd tried like hell to redirect.

She wasn't going to play. Playing wasn't her thing. He needed to remember that. He really did. Turning, he headed down the beach. Not to the party, not yet. He needed a moment—

"Zach?"

Alone. He'd needed a moment alone, away from her, to clear his head, where he couldn't see her looking at him, so sweet and sexy, smiling that smile—

A little breathless, she ran around to the front of him, one hand stopping her loose hair from sliding into her face, the other spread on her dress as if to keep it from blowing up in the wind.

Torn between hoping for a gale-force wind or running away, he stood there instead, rooted to the spot. "You look…"

"Silly, right?" She smoothed down the fabric but the breeze continued to tease the flimsy material, lifting it, revealing her lovely thighs for one all-too-brief, tantalizing glimpse. "I know. I should have stuck with something more practical—"

"Amazing," he managed. Even the sound of her voice lifted his spirits. Somehow she made him feel better by just being. "I was going to say you look amazing."

"Oh." She flashed another kill-him-slowly smile. "It's just a dress."

"I like it. I like the lip gloss, too." It smelled like peaches, and he wondered, if he leaned in right now, would she let him have another taste of her?

Just one.

Who was he kidding? One taste wouldn't cover it. Neither would two. Nope, nothing less than an entire night of tasting would be good enough.

Tipping back his head, he stared up at the star-littered sky, taking a moment to draw in the salty air, to listen to the waves.

But that moment didn't give him the peace he needed. Not when she was still looking at him, her gaze wordlessly telling him that she wanted him, too. "You should head on over to the party." He gestured with a hitch of his chin to the bonfires already going about a hundred yards down the beach, and the growing crowd.

In spite of what Zach thought of him, the new chief was extremely popular.

"Can we walk first?" Brooke gestured in the opposite direction. "Just us?"

Walking alone with her on a moonlit night along the beach? A fantastically bad idea.

"Please?"

No. Absolutely not.

She held out her hand. "Sure," his mouth said without permission from his brain, and taking her hand, he led her down the path to the water. There they kicked off their flip-flops and walked with the surf gently hitting the shore on their right, the cliffs on their left and the moonlight touching their faces.

Pretty damn romantic, which didn't help.

A wave splashed over their bare feet and legs, and the bottom of Brooke's dress got wet, clinging like plastic wrap.

Perfect. Just what he needed. Brooke all wet.

Letting out a low laugh, she gathered the material in her hands, pulling it up above her knees as she backed farther up on the sand.

He thought she'd turn and head toward the party, but she didn't. She kept going.

And like a puppy on a leash, he followed.

"It's beautiful, isn't it?" she asked.

He took in her profile, the small smile on her glossed lips, the few freckles across her upturned nose, her hair flying around her face. "Yes," he agreed. "Beautiful."

Her gaze flew to his. "I was talking about the scenery."

"I know."

"But you weren't looking at it."

"No."

"I…" She let out what sounded like a helpless sigh. "You were saying that I'm beautiful?"

"Yes."

"See, that's the thing."

"There's a thing?"

"Well, you make me feel a thing." She looked away. "A few things, actually."

Uh-huh. And that made two of them.

The breeze continued to toy with the wet hem of her dress and his mind at the same time. He took in the empty beach, the myriad alcoves and cliffs lining the shore, forming lots of private little spots where they could escape to without being seen.

Where he could slowly glide that dress up her legs and—

"Ouch." She hopped on one foot, then bent to pick something up. "A shell."

He traced his finger over it in the palm of her hand. "I used to have jars and jars of these when I was little."

"You grew up here?"

"Yep. Santa Rey born and bred. My parents were surfers. I think my first words were surf's up."

She laughed, but then the sound faded. "You miss them. Your parents."

Lifting his eyes from the shell, his gaze collided with hers. "It was a long time ago, but yeah. I miss them."

"I lost my dad before I was even born, and I still miss him."

"What happened?"

"He died in a car wreck. My mom…she didn't really recover. She never settled in one place again, or with one man."

"That must have been rough on you."

"Not as rough as losing both parents." She squeezed his hand.

Yeah, it'd been rough. He and his parents had lived in an old apartment building on the beach. It'd been run-down, but it had fed their surf habit. He'd remembered every second of the night their building had caught fire. Every second of hearing his mother scream in horror at being stuck in the kitchen, surrounded by flames. Every second of watching his father battle those flames to try to get to her. The fire department had been volunteer at the time. They'd done the best they could, but their best hadn't been enough to save his parents. Their rescue effort had been a recovery effort pretty much from the start.

"Your older brother raised you?"

"He did."

"Does he live here, too?"

"No, Caleb's a high-powered attorney in L.A. Driven and ambitious…we're very different." He smiled. "He's still after me to do something with my life."

"Firefighting isn't doing something?"

He shrugged. "Well, it's not going to get me fame and fortune, or into a cushy old-age home."

"You don't care about any of that."

"No."

She nodded, looked down at her fingers, then back into his eyes. "We're very different, too. You and I."

"I know."

"Are you okay with that?"

Zach felt a smile tug at his mouth. "I happen to like the differences between a man and a woman."

She let out a soft laugh. "I meant that you're laid-back and easygoing, and I'm…not."

"I don't judge my friends."

"Yeah, about that." Her gaze dropped to his mouth. "I have a question."

He hoped like hell it was something like, *Can I kiss you again?*

She hesitated, then shook her head. "I need to walk some more."

"Okay." But he was saying this to her back because she'd already started walking, not along the water this time, but up the sand toward the bluffs, where they could move over rocks the size of houses. She did just that, climbing one, reminding him that she was a capable, strong woman who spent her days lifting heavy gurneys.

He followed behind her, enjoying the way her dress bared her back, her arms, how it kept catching between her legs.

With a huff of frustration, she finally hiked the dress to midthigh so she could move easier, a sight he greatly enjoyed from his lower vantage point.

Her panties matched her dress.

Then she vanished from view. "Brooke?"

"Up here."

He found her on a ledge the size of his pickup truck, sitting with her arms wrapped around her knees, her face turned out to the ocean, the waves tipped in silver from the moonlight. "Isn't it amazing?" she whispered.

Yeah. Yeah, it was, but she was even more so. He sat next to her so that their shoulders touched, and for a long moment neither of them spoke.

"The waves are mesmerizing." She sighed. "I could watch them all night."

"You should see them beneath a full moon."

"I've rarely taken the time to just sit and watch waves. Actually, that's not true. I've *never* taken the time to just sit and watch waves." She let out a long breath and looked at him.

"You had a question," he reminded her.

A ghost of a smile crossed her lips. "I was thinking maybe I'm too rigid. For instance, I shut down this thing between us without giving it full consideration. I said I wanted a relationship, but the truth is, I'm leaving in a matter of weeks. I couldn't really have a relationship, anyway. Plus, you were right about me not relaxing enough. Letting loose. I need to try some of that." She paused and looked at him for a reaction.

"Okay," he said carefully. "So…"

"It's just that I'm not exactly sure how to start." She flashed an insecure smile. "I've always been in school, or working. It's not really left a lot of time for anything else. I mean, I've had feelings for guys before, of course, but…but not in a while. A long while, actually." She paused again. "Do you understand?"

He was trying.

With a sigh, she took his hand. "I'm attempting to come on to you." She brought his hand up to her chest, over the warm, creamy skin bared by her halter dress to her heart.

He looked down at his long, tanned fingers spread over her, feeling the curve of her breast beneath his palm, and the way her heart beat wildly, and then stared into her eyes.

"Just once," she said very softly, "I want to be wild and crazy without worrying about anything. No meaning, no strings, no falling for anyone, just…let loose."

"I want to be very clear," he said, just as softly. "You're looking to—"

"Have sex."

"Have sex." She wanted to have sex. Just once. Had she been dropped here by the fantasy gods? How the hell had a shit-spectacular day turned so perfect?

"Zach? Am I doing this wrong?"

He let out a low laugh—it was for real. "You're not doing anything wrong, believe me. But…" He looked around them, at the rock. "Now?"

"Yes, please."

Again, he laughed. *Laughed.* "Here?"

"Here."

His entire body reacted to the thought, so apparently he was on board with the here and now.

"Just the once," she clarified.

"To be wild and crazy."

She smiled. "That's right. And no falling. No messy emotions. Promise me."

"No falling. No messy emotions." He was so ready, his board shorts had gotten restricting, but he hesitated. "Brooke. What if that doesn't work?"

"Well, of course it'll work. We'll take our clothes off and lie on them, and then—"

He interrupted with a smile. "Trust me, I know how to do *that* part. I meant, what if once isn't enough? What if we still go up in flames when we look at each other at work? What if afterward, someone gets hurt?"

"Won't happen," she said so firmly that he was momentarily stymied by the fact that she was so sure she wouldn't want him again. "You just promised me no falling," she said. "I promise it right back. I'll be leaving town before I can start worrying about any sort of meaningful relationship."

True, all true, but…

"Besides, I'm not exactly the type to ignite any sort of wild passion, so—"

"Whoa." He was still reeling from her certainty that she would get him out of her system so easily. *"What?"*

She lifted a shoulder. "I'm awfully buttoned-up, Zach. Ask anyone."

"I'm asking you."

"It's years ingrained. Far too long a story to tell you now, but—"

"Give me the CliffsNotes version, then." This he had to hear. Not the type to ignite wild passion? Was she serious?

"I just put the prospect of sex on the table," she said. "And you want to talk? See? Proof right there that I don't ignite passion."

"Oh, don't worry. We're going to have sex on the table. Or on the rock." He smiled when just the words brought a blush to her cheeks. "But first I want to hear the long Brooke story."

"Really?"

She sounded so surprised that it squeezed his heart. Had no one ever bothered to try to get beneath her skin? "Really."

"Well…you already know I came here from back East."

"Boston. And before that, Florida."

"You remembered."

"I'm a good listener."

"And a good cook. And a surfer. And—"

"This is about you," he reminded her.

"But see, that's my point, Zach. I'm not good at a bunch of things like you are. I've never had the time to be. Before college, I lived in South Carolina. Before that, New York. Before that, Virginia. Before that…so many other places I can't even remember them all."

"Because your mom liked to move around a lot after your father died."

"Yeah."

So Brooke had been dragged around like a rag doll, with no say in her life until she'd been on her own. No wonder she liked her careful control. "Sounds tough."

"It doesn't matter—this isn't a poor-me story. My point is, I got my uptight analness from my childhood, or lack thereof, but I could be worse, and yes, I realize you're thinking that'd be quite a feat, but it's true. In any case, I've led a sort of wanderlust life."

"When all you really wanted was stability. Comfort."

Again, she revealed surprise that he got her. "Yes. And then my grandmother died and shocked everyone by leaving me her great big old house, chock-full of sixty-plus years of stuff, even though she didn't know me. I shouldn't have cared, but I did. I couldn't just let strangers box it up and get rid of it."

"Of course not."

She looked around, at the rock, the ocean, gesturing wide. "So here I am."

"So here you are. In a house. A home, actually. That's probably new to you."

"Very." She lifted a shoulder. "At least for another few weeks, until the job's over, and the house sells. It's going on the market this weekend." She met his gaze, and in hers the truth was laid bare. No matter what happened, despite the danger of caring too much, or falling a little too hard, she didn't want to miss out on this.

Neither did he. The wind kicked, stirring the warm evening. Her bare arm bumped his, a strand of her hair slid along his jaw as he slowly pulled her closer.

She tipped her head up to his, eyes luminous as her hand came up to his chest. She waited until their mouths nearly touched before she held him off. "I'm going to let loose tonight, Zach." Her fingers dug in, just a little. "Consider yourself warned."

His pulse leaped. So did other parts of his anatomy. "I think I can handle it."

"Sure?"

"Very," he murmured, stroking a hand down her hair, her back, cupping her sweet ass and scooting her a little closer, closing his eyes when her mouth brushed over his jaw, then met his.

Oh, yeah. He ran his hands down her body, half braced for her to come to her senses and stop him.

Any moment now…

Instead, she kissed him just the way he liked to be kissed, long and deep and wet, and raw, helpless pleasure flooded him.

And instead of her coming to her senses, he lost his.

9

AT ZACH'S RESPONSE to her kiss—a thrillingly low, rough sound from deep in his throat—Brooke melted and kissed him again, and then again…

"Brooke."

Lifting her head, she looked into his eyes.

His breathing had gone uneven, and against her body she could feel his, solid and warm and…hard.

Very hard.

She put her hand to his chest and felt the solid thudding of his heart. "Don't change your mind."

"No." Eyes hot, a low laugh escaped Zach. "No. But we could go to my place, or—"

"No." She wanted another kiss. She loved the way he tasted, the way he smelled, so innately male she could hardly stand it. How long since she'd felt this way? Too long, that's all she knew. "Right here. It'll help me relax, Zach. I really need to relax."

Laughing silkily, he slid his hands to her waist, squeezed, then let them glide up her ribs, stopping just before her breasts. Her aching breasts. "Anything to help," he murmured, leaning in to kiss her again.

That worked. So worked. He wanted her. She could feel it in the tension in his broad shoulders, in the taut muscles of his back. Knowing it gave her a heady rush of power, and she demanded more, pressing closer.

His hands slid down her back, pulling her onto his lap, making her momentarily lose concentration as she tried to remember—did she have on pretty panties?—but then she couldn't think at all because his hands were skimming beneath her dress and were on those panties, and he let out another of those sexy rough sounds…

Oh yeah, letting loose worked. She should have tried it a long time ago. Already it was beating back the inexplicable loneliness she hadn't been able to put a name to. With Zach, she never felt alone; it was part of his appeal. He fascinated her. He had from the start. He was such a presence, so virile, so physical—especially right this minute.

"Brooke?"

He wore his intense firefighter face, or maybe that was just his intensity, period, but mixed in with it was need and desire, stark, glorious desire—for her. "Yes?"

His eyes were on hers as his hands continued to mess with her mind. "What are you wearing beneath this dress?"

"Not much."

The sound he made gave her another heady rush, and she gripped the hem of his T-shirt. Helping her, he tugged it over his head, then pulled her back in. The full physical contact made her hum, and then his fingers played with the tie at the back of her neck, the only thing holding up her dress, and the breath evaporated in her lungs.

"Your skin is so soft." He was touching as much of it as he could, running his hands up and down her sides, her arms, her back, under her dress, pressing his face to her throat. "And you smell so damn good…"

He smelled good, too. So good she leaned in and put her mouth to his shoulder, opening it on him because she needed a taste, just a little teeny tiny taste—

He sucked in a breath when she bit him.

"Sorry," she managed behind a horrified laugh when he lifted his head. "I'm sorry. I couldn't help it, I just had to—"

The words backed up in her throat as the front of her dress slipped to her waist. He immediately filled his hands with her breasts. "Sorry," he murmured, repeating her words. "I couldn't help it, I just had to."

She would have laughed again but his thumbs slowly rasped over her nipples, and any laughter vanished. Unbelievable. She was closer to an orgasm than she'd been during the last time she'd actually had sex. "Zach…"

"Relaxing yet?" His voice was low, silky.

"T-trying."

"Good. You keep trying." Bending her back over his arm, he dragged hot, wet, openmouthed kisses down her throat and across a breast, and sucked her into his mouth.

At the feel of his tongue stroking her nipple, she gasped, and then again when he settled her so that his erection pressed against the core of her.

He felt hard, very hard. And big. She looked into his glittering eyes, gulping as his hands slid down her thighs, then up the backs of them to play with the edging of her panties.

Oh, God. This was happening. They were doing this. She untied his board shorts.

He hooked his thumbs in the sides of her panties.

She tugged his shorts down, freeing the essentials.

He repeated the favor with her panties and slipped his hardness between her legs, using the rough pad of one finger to stroke her.

She quivered. "Zach—"

He did it again, adding a second finger, and she tightened her legs on his hand so he couldn't stop, because if he did she was going to die.

"I won't stop," he promised, reading her mind, playing in the slippery heat he'd generated, a heat she'd forgotten existed.

"Condom," she managed.

He went utterly still, then pressed his forehead to hers. "Christ. I don't—Brooke. I didn't think about—"

"I have one."

His gaze, so steamy hot it singed everything it touched, met hers.

"In my purse. It's been there for a while…" She fumbled for the zippered compartment. "I wish I had two—"

His laugh was soft and sexy as he took it from her fingers. "This'll work for now."

Biting her lower lip, she nodded, touching his chest, his flat abs, and then lower still, where his shorts were opened.

He stopped breathing.

So did she.

Bold in a way she hardly recognized, she wrapped her fingers around him. Loving the way that made him let out a rough oath, she slowly stroked. Swearing again, he slid the skirt of her dress up to her waist, baring her to the night and his searing gaze.

"Um…"

"Relaxed yet?"

"Not quite, no." Her dress was now bunched across her

belly, leaving her hanging out in the wind. Literally. Relaxed? Try wound up tighter than a coil.

"Lie back, Brooke."

Doing so would pretty much spread her out like a feast. "Yeah, but—"

He merely laid her back himself. Towering over her, he slid a leg between hers and glided his hands down her arms to join his fingers with hers. "How about now? Relaxed now?" he murmured, pulling their entwined hands up, over her head.

Was he kidding? She was so far from relaxed she couldn't even remember the meaning of the word. He was holding her down in the dark, only the moonlight slashing across his face, making him look like a complete stranger. But instead of the logical response of panic, she arched up against him, wanting more.

He gave it to her. Lowering his mouth to within a fraction of hers, he nipped at her lower lip, then danced his tongue to hers, long and sure and deep, and she gave back everything she got.

She was a different woman with him, someone who let herself live and love. And she wanted to be loved, more than she'd imagined. Closing her eyes, she rocked into him, moving impatiently against him, her fingers digging into the muscles of his back. "Zach, please."

"I plan to. I plan to please you until you—"

"Relax?"

"Come." He slid down her body, kissing her stomach, her ribs. "And then again." Making himself at home between her thighs, he smiled wickedly. "And again."

Oh, God. If he kept at it, she was going to go off in approximately two minutes—

He gave a slow, sure stroke of his tongue and she revised her estimation to two *seconds*. His hands skimmed up her legs to her inner thighs, holding her right where he wanted her, and then he added a finger to the mix and she couldn't have stopped from exploding to save her life. It hit her like a freight train, and he made her ride it out to the very end, slowly bringing her down…

After a moment, or maybe a year, she came back to her senses and realized she lay there on the rock, staring up at the stars, her hands fisted in Zach's hair, holding him to her in a way that would have horrified her if she'd been capable of rational thought, which she wasn't. Not quite yet.

He pressed his lips to one inner thigh, then the other, then crawled up her body, his mouth trailing hot and wet kisses along her skin as he went. She ran her hands up and over his back, his shoulders, and he let out a quiet sound of pleasure.

Taking her face in his hands, his mouth came back on hers as he pushed inside her, filling her so that she thought she might burst, holding her there on the very edge with fierce thrusts that sent pleasure spiraling through her, so far beyond anything she could have imagined. They never stopped kissing, not until the end when she fell apart for him again, and when he did the same for her, his head thrown back, her name on his lips.

When it was over, he rolled to his back so that they lay there on the rock side by side, breathing like lunatics, staring up at the stars, listening to the ocean crashing onto the sand just below them.

"That was…" She let out a half laugh. Words failed.

"Yeah." His voice was husky, rough. "That was."

Turning her head, she looked at him and felt her heart

catch at the sight of him, all long, defined grace, lit only by the silvery moon, which was a good color for him. Hell, any color would be good for him with that mouth-watering body.

Shifting to his side, he smiled as he reached for her and pulled her against him.

A cuddle.

Damn it, he really knew the moves, didn't he. Hard to keep her distance with him, that was for sure. But she was letting loose, so what the hell. Brooke scooted in as tight as she could get, loving the steady thud of his heart beneath her ear, loving the warm strength of his body all around hers, loving the feel of his hands skimming over her. "Maybe we should get up before we forget we only had the one condom."

His answer was a soft laugh, and he pressed his mouth to her ear. "There are plenty of ways around that."

She stared into his naughty, bad-boy smile, a smile that assured her that whatever *ways* he had in mind, she was going to like them. Her body was already halfway to another orgasm at just the thought. "The party."

"Yeah." He let out a breath. "Right."

"I mean, we should go, right? Blake said you need the kiss-up points with the chief." She sat up, looking for her panties, which were behind them, lying on top of his shorts. It was silly, given what they'd just done, but it looked so intimate. Too intimate. Snatching them both, she tossed him his shorts, and watched him pull them on that body she could happily look at unclothed for hours.

Days.

Weeks.

Oh, God. So much for keeping her head.

She spent the next few awkward seconds trying to right her dress, and not having much luck until he turned her away from him and tied her halter himself. "Brooke?"

Just the sound of his voice did her in. Closing her eyes, she swallowed hard. "Yeah?"

Zach stroked a finger down the back of her neck, evoking a shiver and a yearning that weakened her knees again. "I loved watching you let loose."

"Twice."

He grinned as he pulled on his shirt. "I still think we should try for a perfect hat trick."

"Party," she said weakly, tempted to do just that. "We're going to the party."

THEY WALKED down the beach toward the party together, Brooke's mind working overtime. The hot, sexy guy walking alongside her had seen her naked.

Touched her naked.

Kissed her naked—

"Well, well. What do we have here?"

Brooke jerked her thoughts to the present and looked at Cristina, who stood in front of them on the sand in a tiny bikini top and a pair of board shorts riding low on her trim hips. "You two look quite...*flushed* this evening."

Just behind her, the chief's birthday bash appeared to be in full swing. There was a big bonfire and several barbecues going. Music blared out of a set of speakers, and people were sitting on the sand, standing around the fire or dancing. Aidan was swaying like peanut butter on jelly with a pretty brunette. Dustin and Sam were happily flipping burgers. Blake was adding logs to the fire.

There were a bunch of other people, as well, from different shifts and different firehouses. In the center, enjoying the attention, stood Chief Allan Stone himself. A tall man in his fifties, he had the air of an army general and commanded respect—even fear—on the job. But tonight he was smiling and looking more comfortable than Brooke had ever seen him.

But mostly all she could see was the cynical twist to Cristina's lips as the female firefighter took the time to scrutinize Brooke from head to toe.

Brooke could only imagine what she looked like, and shifting uncomfortably, glanced down at herself. Yep, her dress was a wrinkled mess, not a surprise given that ten minutes ago it'd been rucked up to her waist.

Zach reached out and pulled something from her hair. A piece of dried seaweed. Perfect.

"I'd call the cute police," Cristina said dryly, "but they wouldn't know who to arrest first." And with that, she turned and walked back to the fire.

"She knows," Brooke whispered.

Well, she wouldn't go back and change it even if she could. She'd be remembering tonight for many, many nights to come, and would undoubtedly get all hot and bothered all over again at the remembering, and maybe even ache over what might have been, but she wouldn't take it back.

"Ready?" he asked.

She nodded, and they joined the crowd. Zach was immediately pulled away and put on barbecue duty, leaving her standing on the outskirts, a little bit anxious. Which was ridiculous. She'd just been bare-ass naked on a rock, she sure as hell could handle this.

Dustin came up to her and offered a plate of food.

He waited until she'd taken a big bite of the burger. "Hungry, huh?"

She slid him a glance. "Yes."

He nodded and said nothing else. Just stared a little glumly at the dance floor where Cristina was dirty dancing with someone Brooke had never seen before. "Why don't you ask her to dance?" she asked.

"Because she'd think it was funny."

"Funny that you have a crush on her?"

"I don't have a crush on her." He sighed. "Okay, I do. *Shit*."

Sam and Eddie brought Brooke a drink. "To replenish the fluids," Sam explained. Both men looked at her expectantly.

"What?"

"You tell us," Eddie said.

Instead, she took another large bite of her burger.

"Don't you have anything you want to share?" Sam looked hopeful. "With your two best friends?"

"We're best friends?"

They both nodded eagerly. "So if something was on your chest," Sam said. "And you just needed to, you know, get it off—"

"In detail," Eddie added. "We're all ears."

Her burger congealed in her gut. "You know?"

"Oh, we know all."

She looked at Dustin, who grimaced, then nodded. She handed him back the plate, and Eddie the drink, and then walked off. She stopped at the water's edge.

"Stop sulking, will you?"

Brooke turned and faced Cristina. "I'm not sulking."

"Pouting, then. Look, this is a fire station. We're all

walking God complexes who put our lives on the line every day, and yet socially? Immature as high school kids. Come on—" she snorted when Brooke scoffed "—we love to talk. You've given us something new to talk about. Deal with it."

Brooke sighed. "How long will it last?"

"Until it's over."

"It is over."

"Please."

"It is. It was a one-time-only thing."

"Okay, now I *know* you're crazy."

"Why?"

"Why would you sleep with that man only once? That's just a waste of all that hotness."

"I'm leaving in a few weeks. We agreed it was just a letting-loose thing."

Cristina stared at her, then laughed. "And let me guess. You're already regretting that stupid decision."

Brooke looked away, into the bonfire. "No." *Yes.*

Cristina just shook her head. "Well, lucky for me, your shortsightedness is another woman's gain." And she walked away in her sexy little top and shorts, heading directly toward Zach, stopping to hug Blake.

Zach stood at one of the barbecues, holding a long spatula, flipping burgers and laughing at something Aidan was saying to him. Just looking at him, something happened inside Brooke. A clutch. A quiver.

What would it be like if she wasn't leaving? she wondered.

But she always left.

Always.

Besides, she'd said no strings. She'd insisted. She'd

come here tonight, just wanting to let go, to live and, oh boy, had she. She just hadn't realized that in doing those things, something else would happen.

In spite of her promise, she'd begun to fall for Zach.

She watched as Cristina took the plate out of his hands and handed it to Aidan before drawing Zach over to where people were dancing, proceeding to grind up against him in tune to the music.

"Here."

Brooke stared down at the proffered beer, then into Blake's face.

"You looked like you could use it," the tall, thin firefighter said gently.

"I…"

"Drink. Then we'll dance. If it makes you feel better, you can rub all over me like she is with Zach. I'm a good friend like that."

"I'm not jealous or anything."

"Okay."

"I'm not."

He just nodded.

And she drank the beer, then took him up on his offer to dance.

10

After dancing with Cristina, Zach moved to the coolers to get a drink. He pulled out a soda, then stood there with the waves at his back, looking for Brooke.

She'd been dancing with Blake, but now was with Sam, who was making the most of his time with her. Twice the firefighter's hands slipped to her ass, and twice Brooke lifted them to her waist.

Sam grinned in a can't-blame-a-guy-for-trying way, and Zach considered going over there and tossing him into the ocean, but he didn't.

An hour ago, Brooke had been in *his* arms, panting his name as she came all over him. She'd let loose now. Washed him right out of her system and that was fine. Hell, that was great. He'd just move on, too, and—

"You holding up?" Tommy asked, stopping next to Zach, sipping a beer.

"Why wouldn't I be?"

"Haven't heard from you in a few hours. Couldn't figure out if I should be worried, or if it was because you were finally trusting me to do my job."

Zach let out a long breath. "And how is that going? Your job?"

Tommy just took a drink.

"Shit. Don't tell me it's not going."

"I'm not saying that. I'm not saying anything."

"Well, then, say something."

"You're just going to have to trust me a little bit longer."

Unfortunately, he really had no choice. Tommy walked away, and Zach watched Brooke dance some more. Her cheeks were flushed, her hair a little wild. She'd definitely loosened up tonight, and he couldn't tear his gaze off her. Forcing himself to, he moved to stand by Blake, who was back at the bonfire.

The other firefighter tossed a log into the flames, watched it catch. "You could just ask her to dance."

"Who?"

Blake shook his head in disgust, then tossed another log into the fire before swiping a forearm over his sweaty brow. He didn't look so good, and Zach frowned. "You okay?"

"Yeah."

"Why don't you take a break, let me relieve you for a few?"

"I've got it."

Blake had been quiet and down all year since Lynn had died. Of all of them, Zach thought maybe he at least knew a little of what he was feeling. "Blake—"

"I said I'm good."

Great. They were both good.

And they were both liars.

For Zach, the next few days whirled by, a blurry, crazy merge of calls. He didn't sleep well, and finally gave up even trying, ending up at the firehouse kitchen table with his laptop, going through all his gathered arson information to distract himself from daydreaming about the feel of Brooke's curves, the taste of her skin…

And then the object of his fantasies walked into the room.

She was early for her shift, looking a little sleepy and a whole lot sexy as she headed directly toward the coffeepot on the counter.

They hadn't had a chance to speak alone since she'd worn that pretty dress with her hair down, her body soft and giving and sweet.

So goddamn sweet.

Her mouth was still soft and sweet now, but she was back in the uniform, complete with her hair all carefully pulled back.

Buttoned-up.

It didn't matter. He remembered what she looked like with her hair down, not to mention without her clothes, and he wanted to undo her all over again.

He wanted that. *He,* the one who'd not wanted a relationship.

Jesus. He really needed more sleep.

Brooke doctored herself some coffee, then looked at him. "What are you doing?"

Since the answer to that was, "something I shouldn't be," he shut the laptop.

"You and Blake. I caught him looking at porn, too."

"Excuse me, but I was *not* looking at porn."

Over her mug, she raised a brow. "What was it Viagra Man said? Guys will be guys?"

"For God's sake." He opened the laptop back up. "Come here and look for yourself."

"Oh no, thank you." She was laughing now, and lifted her free hand. "What you do in your own spare time—"

Reaching out, he grabbed her hand and tugged her over, letting go just before she fell right into his lap, where he really wanted her.

She sat in the chair next to him and looked at him for a long beat; he looked back.

"Hi," she whispered.

He smiled. "Hi."

Turning her head, she stared at the screen, at the list of property deeds and the records of ownership he'd been studying, and her smile faded.

"The fires," she said quietly. "The arsons."

"Yeah. Doing some research." Which was getting him nowhere. Nothing matched. None of the current owners, none of the past owners, none of the three properties were related to each other in any way. After all these weeks, he was at an impasse, and was afraid Tommy was, too.

"You're trying to link them together."

He wasn't supposed to be doing any such thing. He certainly shouldn't be discussing it.

"What about the way the fires were started?" she asked.

They'd all been started in a wire-mesh trash can, with a second point of origin as bait for the investigator to find and be misdirected, but he was afraid he was the only one who knew that. "Similar," he admitted.

"Suspects?"

He stared at her. She wasn't lecturing him on how stupid it was to risk his job digging into this. She wasn't telling him all the reasons why these fires hadn't been arson. She was sitting here, believing him, believing *in* him. "Most arson is committed by the owners. But the owners of these properties aren't connected in any way that I can see."

"New structures? Or old?"

"Newer."

"What about contractors, then?"

"All different."

"Okay, then. Back to location." Standing up, Brooke paced the length of the kitchen and back again. Leaning in over his shoulder, she typed on the keys of the laptop. "If we compare their footprints…"

He couldn't stop staring at her, bowled over by her analytical mind, her quick thinking. "I already did."

"And?"

And her scent was extremely distracting. As was the way her breast gently pressed into his arm. "They were all different square footage," he told her. "Different building types. Different everything."

"Show me."

He brought up the map he'd created. Her arm was resting on his shoulder. Her skin looked so damned silky, and he knew from experience that she tasted amazing.

Everywhere.

"There's got to be a connection." She was studying the screen, her brow furrowed, her mouth grim. "Somewhere."

She believed in him. The knowledge was staggering. "Brooke."

"Somebody is connected in some way. An employee, a relative, someone…" She was thinking, chewing on her lower lip, eyes still glued to the screen, and he couldn't take his off her.

"Maybe—"

"*Brooke.*"

Her gaze cut to his questioningly.

And he lost his breath. Instead of talking, he tugged on her hand, so that she was forced to lean in closer until she lost her balance.

He caught her.

And then he kissed her.

With a soft murmur, she wrapped her arms around his neck and kissed him back. Oh yeah, *this* was what he'd needed for days—hell, maybe his entire life—and he kissed her until they had to break apart to breathe.

They were still staring at each other when the kitchen door opened and Aidan walked in. "Hey."

Brooke leaped back to her chair like a Mexican jumping bean.

"Anyone got food?" Aidan asked.

"Uh…" Brooke put her hands to her cheeks. "I have cookies on the top shelf."

"Score." Aidan helped himself while Brooke rose to her feet.

"Gotta clock in," she said and, with a last glance at Zach, left the room.

Zach thunked his head to the table.

"What?" Aidan took two fistfuls of cookies and plopped himself down next to Zach, peering at the laptop. "Trying to link them." He nodded. "Hey, maybe if you—"

"Aidan."

"Huh?"

He had to laugh. "I was sort of in the middle of something with Brooke."

Aidan blinked. "Oh. You mean…" He pointed a finger at himself. "You wanted me to leave you two alone?"

"Man, you are quick."

"I thought you two already knocked it out."

Zach winced, and Aidan sat back. "Wow."

"What?"

"Nothing."

"Oh, it's something."

"Okay. You're falling for her."

The door burst open again and Brooke stood there looking more than a little ruffled.

Aidan got to his feet. "Apparently I'm supposed to leave you two alone."

Zach rolled his eyes.

Brooke just kept staring at him until Aidan was gone. "Did you know everybody is talking about us? Why is everyone talking about us? It feels like we're twelve and in middle school."

"Since there's sex involved, let's call it high school. Ignore it. It'll blow over."

She glared at him. He couldn't help it; he laughed. "It will."

"You're not bothered at all?" she asked.

"I'm just saying it's what they do. Seriously, it'll all fade away if you just—"

"Yeah, yeah. Let it go. But maybe I'm not like you, all cool and calm and so laid-back that I have to be checked for a pulse."

Before he could say anything to that, she sighed and rubbed her eyes. "I'm sorry. That wasn't fair. I guess I'm still having bad new-kid flashbacks."

He moved toward her and lowered her hands from her face. "We're adults, and we made a decision. A decision that turned out to be the best night of my entire summer. Don't regret it, Brooke. Please don't."

As she looked at him, her eyes softened. Her body softened, too, and she nodded. "It *was* nice, wasn't it?"

"Nice?" He shook his head. "Nice is a walk in the park. Nice is a sweet goodbye kiss. Nice is a lot of things, Brooke, but it doesn't come even close to covering what we did on that rock."

"Okay, so maybe nice isn't quite the right word. How about good? Do you like that word better?"

He looked into her eyes. Beyond the irritation was a light that said she was playing with him now, but he'd show her good. Backing her to the refrigerator, Zach covered her mouth with his, swallowing her little gasp of surprise, a gasp that quickly turned into the hottest murmur of undeniable need and hunger he'd ever heard when his tongue swept alongside hers.

And though he'd meant only to show her up, he ended up showing himself something. That she fit against him as if she'd been made for the spot. That her scent filling his head, and the feel of her hands fisting in his shirt fueled his hunger as she sighed into his mouth, until it became so damn arousing he couldn't bear it. Pulling back, he stroked a hand down her body and felt her knees buckle.

His own weren't so steady, either, but a fierce sense of satisfaction went through him. Still holding her between the refrigerator and his own hard, aching body, he looked down into her face. "Tell me again that that was merely *good.* I dare you."

"Okay." She licked her lips, an action that didn't help calm him down any. "Does shockingly incredible work for you, Officer Hottie?"

He rolled his eyes but could admit that yeah, shockingly incredible worked far better. "So what now?"

"The million-dollar question, Zach? From you? Really?"

He found himself staring at her. Holy shit, had he actually asked, "What now?"

"Yeah," she said into the charged silence. "That's what I thought. There's *nothing* now. Both of us know it. We just have to remember it."

LATER THAT DAY, after having been out for hours on a series of nonemergency transport calls, Dustin and Brooke were directed to a familiar address for another Code Calico.

"How about you take it this time," Brooke said to Dustin.

He looked amused. "You catch on quick."

"I try."

"You're trying a lot of things lately. Or people. What?" he said innocently when she sent him a long look. "Just wondering about the status."

"I'm not asking you the status of *your* love life."

"Ha!" He grinned victoriously. "So you admit there *is* a love life."

They arrived on scene, mercifully saving Brooke from having to answer, since she didn't know the answer. The truth was, she no longer knew anything at all about what she and Zach were doing. Stepping out onto the sidewalk, she craned her neck, searching the three large trees out in front of Phyllis's place for the cat.

No Cecile in sight.

"Dustin," she said, watching as Aidan and Zach pulled up, moving with steady purpose toward the house, not the yard. "What's going on?"

Dustin put the radio mic back in its place, his expression suddenly serious. "It's not Cecile after all. Grab your bag."

For a split second, she stared at his back as he headed to the front door, then grabbed her bag and ran after him.

Inside the house, the shades were drawn, but she could still see well enough. As her grandmother's place had been, the house was filled to the brim with furniture from another era, upon which knickknacks covered every inch. But there wasn't a speck of dust anywhere, even the wood floors had been shined.

"In here!"

She and Dustin followed Zach's voice down a hallway, its walls hidden by photographs from at least five decades, to a bedroom filled completely with lace. In the center, on the floor, lay Phyllis. Far too still at her feet sat Cecile, gaze glued to her mistress, tail twitching.

Zach was kneeling at Phyllis's side, holding her hand, saying something to her.

Phyllis, eyes closed, responded with a nod. "Yes, Zachie, I can hear you. Tell Cecile I'm okay. She's worried."

"Phyllis, about your meds." Zach spoke calmly, evenly, any personal concern well tucked away, but Brooke could see it in his eyes. "Did you forget to take them?"

"No, I took my damn pills. You hound me enough about it, I don't forget."

"Okay, good." Zach squeezed her hand. "That's good."

Dustin moved in and crouched at her other side, and began taking vitals. Brooke recorded everything, all the while watching Zach be so sweet and gentle and kind.

Why she was surprised, she had no idea. She'd seen him in action before, with many victims by now, and he was always sweet and gentle and kind.

He'd been nothing but those things with her, as well.

And once, on a rock beneath a star littered sky, he'd been much, much more…

When it was determined that Phyllis had to be transported to the hospital, Zach helped get her on a gurney, where the older woman began to panic. "I can't leave. What about Cecile?" Reaching out, she gripped Zach's shirt with an iron fist. "I don't want to go!"

"Phyllis." Zach took both her hands in his. "Your doctor wants you to meet him at the hospital. He wants to stabilize your condition—"

"Condition shmondition. I don't have time for him. I'm fine. Completely fine, I'm telling you."

But she wasn't. Her color was off, her breathing coming too shallow and too fast, and, given the grimace on her face, she knew it, too. "Damn it," she said, sagging back. "Damn it. I'm not going." But she said this much weaker than before. "I'm not. You can't make me."

"Phyllis." Zach stroked back her gray hair as he leaned on the gurney to look into her eyes. "You do this for me and I'll take care of Cecile. Okay?"

"You'll take care of her?"

"I promise."

Phyllis covered her mouth with a shaking hand and nodded. "Your mother would be so proud of you. I hope you know that."

He squeezed her hand. "Just get better." He gestured to Dustin and Aidan, and they carried her out of the bedroom, navigating down the tight, cramped hallway.

Zach looked around Phyllis's room with an unreadable expression. Then, with a sigh, he grabbed the unhappy cat and tucked her into the crook of his arm. Turning to leave, he found Brooke watching him.

As it had since the beginning, their odd connection caused a spark to pinball off her insides, from one erotic zone to another, and all the ones in between—but this wasn't about their crazy physical attraction. Standing there, looking at him, she suddenly knew. It didn't matter that she'd told herself she wouldn't get her heart involved.

It already was.

"You okay?" she whispered.

"Yeah. It's just that she—" Shutting his mouth, he shook his head. Brooke moved closer and put her hand on his arm.

Something went between them at the touch. Not the usual heat but something much, much more.

Yeah, her heart was involved. Big-time.

PHYLLIS RESISTED getting into the ambulance. She wanted to stay home, she wanted her cat, she wanted everyone to get the hell away from her. She even tried a diversion technique.

"There was a man in my yard," she claimed suddenly as they loaded her inside the rig. "Did you see him? He was holding something."

"Phyllis," Dustin said gently. "You're going to the hospital. If not for me and Brooke, then for yourself."

"I recognize his face, I just can't quite place him…"

"It's going to be okay." Brooke sat with her and held her hand. "You're going to be okay. We're just going to the hospital so your doctor can check on you—"

Phyllis shook her head, her eyes cloudy as she struggled to get up. "You people are idiots."

Brooke sighed. "You promised Zach you'd do this, remember?"

The old lady closed her eyes. "Zachie."

"Yes. He gave you his word that he'd take care of Cecile. And you gave him yours that you'd go get checked out."

Phyllis's mouth tightened, but she stopped fighting at least. Zach's name had calmed her down.

Brooke had a feeling Zach had that control over every woman in his life, whether he realized it or not.

"There really was a man in my yard with a blowtorch, or something like one," Phyllis grumbled, sounding more like her old self.

In the back of the unit as she was, Brooke couldn't see out. She met Dustin's eyes in the rearview mirror and he shook his head. He didn't see a man.

Brooke squeezed Phyllis's hand.

The older woman held on with surprising strength as she looked into Brooke's eyes, her own filled with grief and fear. "I really want to stay home."

"You'll go back soon."

"Promise?"

She was so scared. Brooke's throat tightened, burned. If there was one thing she never quite got used to, it was the helplessness she felt over the things she couldn't make better. "Yes," she whispered. "I promise."

AFTER DROPPING Phyllis off in the ambulance bay of the E.R., Brooke and Dustin were called to another transport. The minute they were free again, Brooke tracked down a nurse to find out what she could about Phyllis's condition.

The nurse pulled her chart. "She's in renal and heart failure."

Brooke's brain refused to process that. "What?"

"Yes, the doctor was just with her."

"Oh my God."

"It's been happening for quite a while. Apparently the patient has actually known for months. She'll be staying a while this time."

"But—I promised her she'd be back home soon."

The nurse frowned at her over the chart. "It's not your job to make promises of any kind."

"I…" Brooke knew that, so she had no idea why she'd done so. "I didn't know about her condition."

"Of course not, because you're not her doctor." The nurse looked down her nose at Brooke, reigning supreme. "Do yourself and your future patients a favor and don't make rash promises. Don't make any promises." Spinning on her heels, she walked away.

Brooke staggered to a chair and let her weak legs sink until she was sitting. Renal and heart failure…

"Rough day?"

She looked up at Zach, in full firefighter gear and looking a little worse for wear himself. "Yeah. Rough day." Damn it, she could barely speak past the huge lump in her throat. "But not as rough as Phyllis's."

"So you know."

When she nodded miserably, he sighed and crouched in front of her. He was in her space but in a very lovely way, his big body sort of curled around her protectively, his eyes easy and calm and full of something she hadn't known was missing in her life.

Simple and true affection.

"I've got Cecile at the firehouse," he said. "Happily scratching the furniture and terrorizing the crew."

He'd made a promise and had followed through. For some reason, that got to her. "Zach. I screwed up."

"We all do."

"I promised Phyllis she could go home soon. But—" Her voice cracked and she stopped talking. Had to stop talking because she couldn't stand the thought of breaking a promise. Her past was a virtual wasteland of promises broken by her mother, and she'd made it a rule to never, ever do the same thing.

Zach let out a long breath, then reached for her hand.

"Now's probably not a good time to be nice to me," she managed. Damn it, she hated this. Hated that she'd failed, much less failed a woman she cared about. "When I'm near a breakdown and someone's nice, I tend to lose it."

"You should know I'm not so good with tears."

She pulled her hand free and closed her eyes. "Well, then, you're not going to like what's coming next." Eyes still shut, she felt him shift his weight. When he didn't speak, she figured that he'd left her by herself, which was definitely for the best. With a sigh, she opened her eyes, prepared to be alone.

As she always had been.

But to Brooke's shock, he'd never left her side.

11

ZACH WATCHED Brooke's expression register surprise on top of the pain already there. She'd really believed that he'd walked away. Tears or no tears, he wouldn't have left a perfect stranger, but she'd actually expected him to abandon her. He knew that wasn't a reflection on him, but on her own experiences. People didn't stick in her life.

Odd how he wanted to. "Phyllis wouldn't want you to lose it over her."

"I told her everything would be okay. I *promised* her. But everything isn't going to be okay."

He knew that, too. Heart heavy, calling himself every kind of fool, he sank into the chair next to her and leaned his tired head back to the wall and studied the ceiling.

It didn't matter that he wasn't looking at her. He could still see her; she'd been imprinted on his brain. A body made for his. A mouth that fueled his fantasies. Eyes that destroyed him with every glance. "Promises are a bad idea all the way around."

Especially the one he'd made to her. Not to fall for her. Man, that one was going to haunt him.

"I know."

Brooke still sounded way too close to tears for his comfort. Turning his head, he found her watching him, eyes still thankfully dry. "Don't be too hard on yourself. We all break promises."

"Some of us do it more spectacularly than others."

"I don't know about that."

She stared at him for a long moment. "Zach…I've not handled any of this well."

"This."

"The new job. Making friends at the new job." She lowered her voice. "You."

"What about me?"

"Sleeping with you and thinking I could just walk away. It was supposed to be letting loose, but you should know I'm having some trouble with that whole walking-away portion of the plan. I have no idea how people do the one-night thing, I really don't."

"There was no sleeping involved."

"What?"

"Our night. We didn't sleep. It's an important clarification, because sleeping implies intimacy."

"What we did felt pretty damn intimate," she said.

"Temporarily intimate. There's a difference. Now, if we'd been getting naked every night since…that would be true intimacy." He looked at her, wanting a reaction, but hell if he knew what kind of reaction he wanted, or why he was even going there.

"You agreed readily enough," she reminded him. "And it's what you do, anyway. Light stuff only."

She was watching him carefully, and sitting there in the hospital chair, surrounded by strangers, the scent of antiseptic and people's suffering all around them, she was clearly waiting for him to deny it. And given how he kept baiting her about it, it made sense that she was confused.

But what he wanted didn't really matter. Not when she was out of here in less than two weeks. But apparently his mouth didn't get the message from his brain because it opened and said, "Whatever this is, clearly we're going to drive each other nuts for the next two weeks, so we might as well take it as far as we can."

She blinked. "You mean…"

"Yeah."

At his hip, his pager beeped. Hell. Rising to his feet, he looked down into her still surprised face. "Think about it."

"I…will."

ZACH'S CALL was to an all-too-familiar address for a house fire.

Phyllis's.

When they pulled down her street, his stomach hit his toes. The house was lit up like a Fourth of July fireworks display. The flames were hot, fast and, as it turned out, unbeatable. Even with Sam and Eddie's engine already there, and two others from neighboring firehouses, in less than twenty minutes they'd lost the entire structure.

Afterward, with the crew all cleaning up, Zach slipped inside the burned-out shell. He moved through the clingy, choking smoke, down the blackened hallway where Phyllis's pictures were nothing but a memory. Inside her bedroom, he took in the soot, water and ashes.

And a wire-mesh trash can, tipped on its side.

On the wall above it, black markings flared out, indicating a flash burn. Probably aided by an accelerant.

Just like the Hill Street fire.

And the two before that.

Jaw tight, Zach stared at the evidence, pulling his cell

phone out of his pocket to take a picture, which he e-mailed to both Tommy and himself. This time, whatever happened, he was going to have his own damn evidence, because no way had Phyllis had a wire-mesh trash can in here, not in the lacy, frilly, girly room.

His cell phone rang, and when he saw Brooke's name on the I.D., he experienced a little jolt. *I've thought about it,* he imagined her saying. *Do me, Zach...*

"I just heard about the fire," she said instead, sounding tight and grim. "Zach, when we were taking Phyllis out of the house, she tried to tell us that someone was standing on the edge of her property, watching us. A man with a blowtorch."

His fantasy abruptly vanished. *"What?"*

"She was fighting us, trying to stall, saying whatever she could to get us to let her go back into the house. We didn't listen to her. And now…"

"And now you just might have helped catch a serial arsonist," he said firmly. "If you were here, I'd kiss you again."

She let out a breath. "But what if—"

"Don't kill yourself with the what-ifs," he said. "I've been there. They don't help."

"OLD HEATING element," Tommy told him the next morning when he found Zach waiting at his office. "Shoddy, unreliable, and as we saw firsthand, dangerous. Thank God Phyllis was still in the hospital and not at home."

Zach just shook his head. "This was no more acciden- tal than the Hill Street fire. The trash can—"

"Zach—"

"Look, Phyllis said she saw a guy standing on the edge of her property with a blowtorch."

Tommy sighed and retrieved two Red Bulls from a small refrigerator on his credenza. "I can't discuss the investigation."

Zach declined the caffeine-rich drink. "Thought you were off caffeine."

"Sue me." Tommy drank deep and sighed again. "Just don't tell my wife."

"Tommy—"

"Look, I talked to Phyllis myself this morning. She's incoherent and in and out of consciousness. She doesn't remember a damn thing about yesterday. Not a guy with a blowtorch, or if she had a wire-mesh trash can or not."

"That's the drugs talking."

"That's all we have. The fire was put out, Zach. It was a job well done on our part. No injuries, no fatalities."

And that was the bottom line. Zach got that. He just didn't happen to agree. "It was also arson."

"Goddamn it."

"I suppose your next line is for me to leave this one alone, too."

"Yes," Tommy said very quietly. "It is."

"You got the picture I sent."

"I got the picture."

"You'd better be on this, Tommy."

"You need to go now, Zach."

Yeah. Yeah, he did, before he did something he might deeply regret. Like lose his job.

When he finally got to the fire station and went to the kitchen for something to put in his empty, gnawing gut,

Brooke was there. He'd hoped to see her last night at his place. In his bed. But clearly she'd thought a little too much. He tried to move past her, but she grabbed his arm.

"Brooke, don't." He felt raw. Exposed. If he let her touch him right now, it might make him all the more vulnerable. Pulling free, he backed up a step and came up against the damn refrigerator.

She merely stepped in against him, trapping him there. He could have shoved past her, but he didn't. Her warm, curvy body pressed to his, her eyes wide and open, reflecting her sorrow, her sympathy.

"The house is completely gone?" she asked.

"Yes."

"Was she right about the guy she saw? Was it arson?"

"I believe so."

"Tommy—"

"Told me again to stay out of this."

"Oh, damn. Zach, I'm sorry." She slid her hands up his chest to cup his jaw. "I'm so sorry."

But not sorry enough to have come to him last night. Knowing that, he might have been able to resist what she did next, except he didn't. She pressed her mouth to his cheek, and then to the corner of his mouth, and then, because he'd apparently lost his mind, he turned his head and hungrily met her lips with his.

Reason went out the window. Everything went out the window as he did his best to inhale her whole. She had her arms wound around his neck, her hands fisted in his hair. He had a hand up the front of her shirt cupping her breast over her bra, the other down the back of her pants, when he vaguely heard someone clear his throat behind them.

Shit.

Lifting his head, he locked eyes with Blake over Brooke's head.

"Bad time?" Blake asked drolly.

Brooke squeaked and hid her head against Zach's chest.

"Very bad," Zach said.

Blake gestured to the refrigerator at Zach's back. "But I'm hungry."

With a choked sound, Brooke stepped away from Zach. Without a word, she walked out of the kitchen.

Blake just arched a brow, gesturing to the fridge.

"Jesus." Zach pushed away from the refrigerator and let Blake at it.

THE NEXT NIGHT, off duty and at home, Zach sat at his own kitchen table with all the evidence he had on the arson fires so far spread out on a board laid in front of him. He was trying to connect the dots instead of thinking about Brooke when the doorbell rang.

It was pizza delivery by Aidan. His partner handed off the extra-large, loaded pie and pushed past him to get inside.

"Well, gee," Zach said dryly. "Come on in."

"We've got to talk." Aidan moved into the kitchen and helped himself to a beer in the refrigerator. He twisted off the top, drank deeply, then gave Zach a long look.

"It's not good," Zach guessed.

"It's you. And what you're doing."

"Look, we're both adults. If we decide to go at this until she leaves, it's our business."

Aidan looked confused. "Huh?"

"You're not talking about Brooke?"

"No." Aidan cocked his head. "Although, I did hear some interesting rumors today, which I ignored. Erroneously so, apparently."

"It's no big deal."

"Okay."

"It's just casual."

"Okay."

"But Jesus, the way everyone's going on about it, I might as well marry her."

Aidan's eyes nearly bugged out of his head. "Whoa. The M word? Out of *your* mouth?"

"It's just a word."

Aidan was still eyeing him like a bug on a slide. "Why are you harping on this?"

"Because you are."

"I said okay about twenty minutes ago, dude. It's all you."

Zach opened the pizza box, pulled out the biggest piece and stuffed a bite in his mouth. "Jenny brought me pizza a while back. Hers was better."

"That's because hers came with a hot bod. You boinking her, too?"

"No."

"Then can I boink her?"

Zach sighed. "Why are you here again?"

"To yell at you. But not for the women. I only wish I had half your woman problems."

"Hey, you've had your problems."

"Name one."

"Okay, how about you doing Blake's soap-star-diva sister and not telling him about it."

Aidan winced. "Hey, she wasn't a soap-star diva at the

time. And besides, I was really young and really stupid back then."

"Uh-huh."

"You're unusually testy. You're either PMSing, or those new rumors are definitely true."

"Which are what exactly?"

"That you and Brooke nearly did it up against the refrigerator. Which, by the way, if it's true? *Nice*."

"Do you ever think of anything besides sex?"

"Alas, rarely." Aidan grabbed his own huge piece of pizza.

"Fine. But I don't want to talk about Brooke."

Aidan shot him an amused look. That rankled. "Okay."

"I don't."

"Fine. Let's talk about a little thing called arson. You told Tommy you thought Phyllis's house fire was deliberately set."

"Yes."

"Are you crazy?"

"It *was* arson."

"Okay, but Tommy is the best investigator this town has ever had and you know it, which means he's on it."

Zach opened his mouth to speak, but Aidan stopped him. "And you also know he has the biggest mouth this town has ever seen. Everyone is talking about you."

"So what?"

"So what? You love this fucking job, that's what. You work your ass off. You're one of the best in the whole damn city, and there's a lieutenant position coming up that you're going to take yourself right out of the running for because you won't leave this alone."

"I can't leave it alone."

Aidan sighed. "You're that damn sure?"

Zach pointed to the material he'd been working on.

Twisting one of the kitchen chairs around, Aidan straddled it, steepling his hands over the back and setting his chin on them as he studied the board on the table. After a long moment, he let out a breath. "Mysterious points of origin. Metal trash cans. And now, maybe a blowtorch." He shook his head. "So what now?"

Zach sat heavily and for the first time put words to the terrible thoughts in his head. "I'm not sure. But look at this." He tossed down the photos he'd taken of the razed properties.

Aidan shifted through the pictures. "Who ordered the demolitions?"

"I'm working on that."

Aidan finished his beer, silent.

"I know. I'm crazy." Zach shoved his fingers through his hair. "I feel crazy."

"No." Aidan shook his head. "Someone is systematically destroying evidence. Tommy either knows this, or…"

They stared at each other at the unspoken implication that Tommy could be behind any of it.

"You're not crazy," Aidan said. "And you need to get to Phyllis before someone convinces her to destroy any more evidence we can use."

"We?"

"Partners," Aidan said. "For better or worse."

LONG AFTER Aidan had left, Zach stood on his back deck, staring out at the night, his mind whirling.

Arson.

Brooke.

Restlessness…

He was surrounded by the life he'd chosen, a life both exhilarating and challenging. He loved it. And yet there was no denying he'd shut himself off from the very thing that people would say mattered most.

Love.

Had he really done that because of losing his family so long ago? Or had it just been an excuse, a handy reason not to let himself get hurt? If so, that had backfired, because he'd gotten hurt, anyway. Whether he was ever with Brooke again almost didn't matter—his emotions were involved.

She hadn't come to him tonight, either. That left him two choices: be alone, or go to her.

Easy enough choice. He went inside and grabbed his keys, and then whipped open the door—to find Brooke standing there, hand raised to knock.

12

BROOKE STOOD on Zach's front steps, having gotten his address courtesy of Dustin. One minute she'd been at her grandmother's, absorbing the sensation of feeling at home inside a house for the first time in…well, ever, and the next, she hadn't been able to stop her mind from wandering to Zach. She had no reason for being here. None.

Okay, that was a lie. She knew. And her body's reaction to the sight of him, all big, bad and slightly attitude-ridden, cemented it.

She was here to, what had he said? Take it as far as they could.

He wore a T-shirt and jeans, no shoes, no socks. Simple clothes.

Not such a simple man. "Hi," she said.

"Hi." He let out a breath and hooked his hand around her elbow, pulling her up the last step and closer to him. In the dim light he was all lean lines and angles and hard muscle as he jangled his keys in his other hand. "I was just coming to see you."

Her heart skipped a beat or two. "You were?"

"Yeah. I got tired of waiting for you to finish thinking." He moved aside so she could come in, but she hesitated.

"Give me a second," she murmured.

"Okay. For what?"

"For my brain to catch up with the rest of me." She smiled nervously. "It's my body that brought me here, you see. For some of that letting loose we're so good at."

He smiled, and her body began to tingle.

"Maybe you should let your body lead on this one," he suggested in a very naughty, silky tone.

"You think?"

"Oh, yeah."

"Just sort of let my brain take a rest?"

"Exactly." Gently crowding her in the doorway, he put his hands on her hips and his mouth to her ear. "So, are you going to come inside?"

"That was going to be my question to you."

His soft laugh stirred the hair at her temple and all her good spots. Then he slid his arms around her and gave her a hug, and along with the lust came such a rush of affection that her heart hurt. She buried her face in his throat and held on tight. "Okay," she said. "Maybe I'll come in for a little while."

"Great idea. We could—"

"Let loose?"

"Anything you want," he murmured, pulling back to look into her eyes. "I wanted to see you tonight."

Her breath caught. "You're seeing me."

"Yeah. I am. I see you, Brooke. The real you."

"With lines like that, you're awfully hard to resist."

"I'm trying to be." Pushing the door shut, Zach kissed her and, turning them both, backed her to the door. This freed up his hands, which he used to cup her face, a touch that turned her on more than any other. "I needed this connection tonight."

"With me?"

"Only with you." He kissed her again, his mouth making its way over her jaw to her throat.

"Zach?"

"Mmm-hmm."

"Zach."

"Right here." His hands slipped beneath her shirt and her eyes crossed with lust.

"I don't have a condom this time. I forgot to put a new one in my purse."

He shoved his hand in his pocket and pulled out…

"Three." Her knees wobbled as she let out a shaky laugh. "Think we can use them all in one night?"

"I have more in my nightstand."

"Oh," she breathed, staring at him.

At her expression, he let out a shaky laugh. "God, Brooke. I don't know what the hell it is about you, but you always make me…"

"What?" She needed to know. "I make you what?"

"Well, it's a bit of a problem." He pressed against her, and she could feel that he did have a problem. A big one.

"Oh my. I see."

"Do you?" His voice was a rough whisper against her ear. "Any ideas?"

"Uh, well, I do have a few. You know, all in the name of assisting a friend in need."

Against her skin, he grinned. "Is that what you're going to do, give me some assistance?"

"I'm a giver, Zach."

He was still laughing when he kissed her this time, and so was she, but his tongue sliding against hers had all that good humor fading away. Pulling up his shirt, Brooke put her hands on his chest, his hard, warm chest, while he lifted her, sandwiching her between his body and the door, rocking into her, and at the sensation, she thunked her head back against the wood, a needy moan escaping her lips as his mouth latched on her neck.

"Love that sound."

So she repeated it, and with a groan, he peeled off her shirt. Beneath she wore only a camisole. He slid the straps off her shoulders, then tugged it to her belly, exposing her breasts. "Look at you," he whispered in awe, leaning in, running his tongue over a nipple then sucking it into his mouth.

She found her fingers in his hair, and tightened her grip, arching up into his mouth. "Now, Zach. Please, now."

Now must have worked for him. He went directly to the button on her shorts while she yanked at his jeans. Somehow, he managed to tear open one of the condoms, and then with their clothes still half on and half off, he slid into her.

Time slowed.

Or stopped.

Or something.

It just felt so right, having him inside her, filling her. It was the only thing that made sense in her unsettled life, the only thing…and she didn't want it to end.

"Brooke." That was all, just her name, as if he felt everything she did. Then he was kissing her, moving within her. Her vision burst into a kaleidoscope of colors, and her blood rushed through her head, roared in her ears. She barely heard herself cry out as she came, or the answering low, strained groan from him as he followed her over.

Lifting his head, he slapped a hand on the door to keep them from hitting the floor. His eyes were dark and sexily sleepy as he looked into her face.

"How was that for some letting go?" she asked, still breathless.

His eyes were still scorching. "If I were to say it wasn't quite enough…?"

"I'd have no choice but to make use of those two other condoms you're carrying."

"Because you're a giver."

"That's right."

They made it to his shower, where Zach smiled down at her in a way that said he was rough and ready, all tough sinew wrapped around enough testosterone to leave her weak in the knees.

His hands were all over her, up and down her back, smoothing her wet hair from her face, skimming her breasts, her hips, her bottom, her thighs, between them…making her groan softly in his mouth, because yeah, his fingers knew her, knew exactly what to do to make her gasp. "Zach—"

"God, you're wet."

She managed a laugh, though it backed up in her throat when he slid a finger into her. "That's because I'm in the shower."

He played that finger inside her, in and then out. "This isn't from the shower."

Before she could respond, he dropped to his knees, pressed her back against the tiled wall and slid his hands up her thighs. "This is from me. You're wet from me." Using his fingers to part her, exposing exactly what he wanted, he leaned in and kissed her, then groaned in pleasure at her taste.

"Me," he repeated thickly, with unmistakable satisfaction.

He was right. Even now, after knowing him in a way she knew few men, he could merely look at her and turn her on.

And his touch…

He wasn't done with her, not even close. "Oh, God," she gasped as he, with gentle, heart-stopping precision, used his tongue, his teeth, his fingers, driving her right to the very edge and holding her there until she gripped his wet hair in her hands, silently begging him to finish her off.

Which he did, and she came again. Exploded, actually. Maybe imploded. She couldn't tell because she departed from her own mind for a few minutes, and when she'd have slipped to the tile in a boneless, orgasmic heap, he caught her. Caught her and surged to his feet, once again pressing her back to the wall, bending his dark, wet head to rasp his tongue over a nipple.

"Wrap your legs around me," he commanded, his voice a low, husky whisper as he lifted his head and impaled her with that dark, direct gaze. "There—God, yeah. There…"

Her breath caught again when he rocked his hips to hers, entering her. He pushed again, going deeper this time, and her entire body welcomed him.

"Don't," he growled when she arched into him. "Don't move, not yet—"

But she couldn't help it, and he swore again as he moved, a slow thrust of those hips, gliding against her sensitized flesh, wrenching a horrifyingly needy whimper out of her as her head thunked back against the wall.

He had his arms low around her hips. One slid up her

back, his fingers slipping into her hair, cushioning her head, protecting it from the tile. "God, you feel amazing." He let out a slow, rough sound of sheer pleasure. "You're so beautiful, so goddamned beautiful…" He thrust into her, wrenching low moans from both of their throats, which comingled in the fogged-up shower as he moved within her…

She'd already come, but she was there again, right there, primed and ready to go, his rhythm knocking her right off her axis. "Zach—"

"I know." Again he bent his head, this time to watch the sight of himself sliding in and out of her body, the pull and tug of their glistening flesh, hers so soft and pliant and wet, his wet, too, but hard, hard everywhere—his chest, his abs, his thighs, between them—

That was it, that was all she took in before her mind went white with blinding pleasure. Vaguely, she felt him follow her over, but she was gone, simply gone.

WHEN SHE COULD breathe once more, Brooke looked into Zach's eyes, which were still dazed enough to stir her up again. She'd wanted to let loose and, oh boy, had she. She'd wanted a change—well, being naked with a man was a huge change. She'd wanted to belong, and she'd found that, too.

She tightened her grip on him so he couldn't move, couldn't break free, not yet, and he pressed his hips to hers as if he didn't want to let go, either.

But then she realized how ridiculous that was. She didn't cling, ever, and she was sure he didn't, so she forced herself to relax her hold, to free him.

But he remained right where he was, muscles still

quaking, eyes still a bit glazed over, just holding her, and something happened to her in that moment, something ripped deep in the region of her chest.

Oh, no. No, no, no…

She was not going to fall in love.

At least not any further than she already had…

Only she wasn't stupid, or slow-witted. She knew the truth. Knew it was far too late. Needing to lighten the mood, she lifted her head and smiled. "Two condoms down…"

He let out a half laugh, half groan.

"Hey, if you're too tired for that third one, I understand."

Eyes glittering at that challenge, Zach bit her lower lip. He then proceeded to teach her a whole new kind of appreciation for her handheld showerhead—and she risked her knees to return the gesture.

By the time they hit his bed and tore open the third condom, she'd "let loose" multiple times and she was one quivering, sensitized nerve ending who could do nothing *but* feel.

And she felt plenty.

So damn plenty.

"Jesus," Zach breathed shakily in her ear some time later. "That third time was…"

"Yeah."

Turning his head, he softly kissed her throat, then her lips, coming up on an elbow to look into her face. "If we don't have the words for it, I say we keep going."

There were many, *many* reasons why she should get up and go home, but there was only one reason why she turned into his arms.

13

ZACH WOKE UP with a hard-on and a smile, both of which vanished when he realized he was alone.

Great. Terrific. Brooke wasn't clingy, and he'd always liked that in a woman. Unable to pinpoint the basis for his sudden irritability, he took a shower, and just looking at the showerhead, remembering its use last night, had him smiling again.

He dressed and stopped to visit Phyllis at the hospital on the way to work. She wasn't awake but he left her flowers and a Polaroid of Cecile sprawled on the firehouse couch, looking like the Queen of Sheba.

The picture reminded Zach that Tommy hadn't called him regarding the photo he'd sent, and something niggled at him, just in the back of his brain, a connection that he couldn't quite put together. It bugged the hell out of him.

At the station, he headed directly for the kitchen and caffeine. He found Cristina raiding someone's lunch and Cecile meowing at her feet for handouts.

Cristina looked at Zach, then did a double take.

"What?" he asked, looking himself over to see if he'd put his pants on backward.

"Hey," Dustin said, coming into the room, gesturing to the sandwich in Cristina's hand. "That's mine."

Cristina took a bite, still staring at Zach. "You know what."

"Not a clue," Zach told her.

"*My* sandwich," Dustin said again.

With a shrug, Zach headed for the coffee, but Cristina muttered something beneath her breath and, frustrated, he turned back to her. "Spit it out then."

She put her hands on her hips. "You're flaunting your just-gotten-laid airs."

"Hello," Dustin said to the room. "Am I invisible? That's my sandwich."

Cristina sighed and handed it over.

Brooke came in but stopped short when she saw them all. A smile slipped out of her at the sight of Zach, one that had *we had great shower sex last night* all over it, and it was adorable.

Cristina saw it and rolled her eyes as Brooke headed to the coffeepot. "Jesus. You two did it *again?* You know it's a dry summer when even the New Hire is getting more than me."

At that, Brooke spilled coffee over the edge of her mug and onto her fingers. *"Ouch."*

"Karma," Cristina told her.

"Hey, Cranky Pants." Dustin tossed Cristina back the sandwich. "Maybe I should go bring you some Wheaties instead."

"I'd rather get lucky."

"You could get lucky," Dustin responded. "Anytime."

"No, I can't." She opened the Baggie and took another bite, still frowning. "My vibrator broke."

Dustin's jaw fell open.

Zach handed him a mug of coffee and gently tapped his chin until his mouth closed. "Easy there, big D."

"Seriously, look at this face," Cristina demanded of Dustin, waving the sandwich around. "Does it say I've gotten any good action lately? Does it say freshly laid? Does it say orgasm central? No, it does not."

Zach glanced at Brooke, who was desperately trying not to look at any of them. He didn't want to brag, but he was pretty damn sure she'd visited orgasm central just last night, compliments of *him*.

Dustin cleared his throat. "You could try a man," he said to Cristina. "You know, instead of a vibrator."

"A *live* penis? Gee, why didn't I think of that?" Cristina poured a pound of sugar into her coffee, stirring so hard some of it splashed out.

Zach leaned in. "A little less anger, you might scare away the penises. Or is it peni?"

She pointed at him. "You, of the Recently Had Sex Club, shut up. You don't get to give me advice."

Brooke went even more red.

"How about me?" Dustin asked. "Can I give you advice?"

"*Hell,* no."

"Why not?"

"I don't take advice from a man who throws his heart into every relationship, only to get it crushed."

"If you don't put yourself out there, then why bother?"

Cristina stared at him as if she'd never seen him before. "You're hopeless. A hopeless romantic."

"You say that like it's a bad thing."

"It's…it's…" But for the first time in, well, history, Cristina seemed to run out of words.

THEIR FIRST CALL of the day came in for a large fire in a warehouse across from the wharf, and all units responded.

By the time Zach and Aidan pulled up, black smoke stretched hundreds of feet into the blue sky like a vicious storm cloud, and the chief was setting up the ICS— Incident Command System. The street was a chaotic mess, making it difficult to get close, but the police were working on directing the civilians out and the fire units in.

Word had come through that there were several people trapped in the warehouse, and Zach eyed the inferno critically. "Not good."

"Going to be tricky," Aidan agreed as they pulled out their equipment.

The chief sent a group of them to the south side of the building, where the missing people had last been seen. Sam, Eddie, Cristina and Blake manned the hoses, while Aidan and Zach prepared to enter the building.

"Now," Blake yelled from the rig, gesturing them in as the gang beat back the flames.

Aidan and Zach went in together, immediately choking on the thick, unrelenting smoke in spite of their protective masks. Visibility was ten feet at first. But only a few yards in, that was cut in half.

"You see red?" Aidan yelled.

"No, but I hear popping like Rice Krispies, so it's coming." In fact, it was earsplitting.

They had no idea where their victims were so Aidan gestured for Zach to go left, and he'd go right. About twenty feet down the dark, smoky hall, Zach heard a woman screaming. "Got one," he said via radio to Aidan, pounding on the doors as he went, stopping at the one from behind which came the screaming.

The wood was hot to the touch.

A door opened behind Zach, and as he turned, a man stumbled right into his surprised arms.

"Claire," the man gasped, and fought to get past Zach. "I hear her, I have to get to Claire!"

The guy was half-unconscious, and the size of a linebacker, an overweight linebacker. Zach gripped him tight, completely supporting his weight. Clearly the guy couldn't go after anyone in his condition. Hell, he couldn't even walk on his own. "You're not going anywhere—"

"I've got to get to Claire! Claire, it's me, Bob! I'm coming!"

"I'll get her."

"No, I—" That's all Bob got out before his eyes rolled up in the back of his head and he slumped to the floor, a dead weight.

Zach hunkered down to sling him over his shoulder, but Bob suddenly came to life, and with what seemed like superhuman strength, grabbed his ankle and tugged.

Zach hit the floor hard.

"Claire!" Bellowing, Bob crawled over him toward the office door.

Zach rolled and managed to hold him down. "You can't go in there. You don't have a mask. I'm taking you out—"

Good old Bob slugged Zach in the gut.

Zach absorbed the blow, using precious oxygen as he got the guy in a choke hold just as the ceiling began crashing down in flaming chunks, one narrowly missing the man's head, and only because Zach yanked him out of the way. "You're wasting time! Wait here—"

"No!" Bob charged for the door, but on the way there, a huge piece of burning tile fell, hitting him hard enough to slam him to the ground, where he finally was still.

Great. Now Zach had to get Bob out and to medical help before he could go for Claire, whose screams were already fading.

Calm but furious, Zach hoisted the man up in the classic fireman's hold and made his way back down the hallway. Luckily, Aidan met him halfway. "Take him," Zach directed. "I'm going back for the woman."

"We've got orders to get out now. The roof's unstable."

No shit. "I can get to her quick." Hands free, Zach turned back. The smoke was even thicker now, pouring in through the walls, making it seem like night. He couldn't see his hand in front of his face.

But worse, Claire was no longer screaming.

Then Eddie and Sam showed up, their lights barely cutting through the darkness. "Zach! Out of here!"

"I know—hold on!" He opened the office door. Behind him he heard Eddie and Sam yelling into their radios for lines of water to come through the office windows and the roof. They were going to get their asses kicked for breaking protocol, but Zach had never been so happy to see them in his life. "Claire!" he yelled as flames roared out the door, right at them, attracted by the new source of oxygen.

From outside, the hoses beat the flames back enough for them to move in; they found Claire crumpled on the floor beneath a desk. Zach dropped down and pulled her toward him. With Eddie flanking one side and Sam the other, he carried her into the hallway, where they were shoved back by flames coming from both directions now.

"Go back the way you came!" came the chief's voice via radio. "Out the way you came!"

They wouldn't make it. They needed a faster way—the office windows. But they couldn't get to them without hoses.

"Do it," Blake shouted into their radio. "I'm on the roof, I'll cover you."

Shocked, they all looked up, and through the burning ceiling, they could see an arc of water coming through.

Blake.

"Hurry!" he yelled down to them. "Move it!"

Eddie went out the window first, straddling the ledge, reaching back for Claire. Sam went next. Waiting until the ladder cleared, Zach took one last look over his shoulder at the flames rushing them, but Blake still had his back.

"Go," Blake shouted as the ceiling started to cave.

"Jesus, Blake!" Zach's heart stopped. *"Get back!"*

"I will when you're out—"

But a thundering shudder silenced them both. Zach made to leap for the ladder, but the ceiling crashed down. As he yelled Blake's name, everything went black.

"Two firefighters are down," Dustin said grimly, setting down the radio.

Brooke's heart stopped. "Oh my God. *Who?*"

Dustin didn't meet her eyes.

She grabbed his sleeve. *"Who?"*

"Blake and Zach." He grimaced, but tried to sound reassuring. "Don't worry, they'll get them out."

"Ohmigod, they're trapped?"

The male victim Aidan had carried out was sitting on the curb holding an ice pack to his head, and at this news, he moaned. "It's my fault. I freaked out. And now Claire's trapped in there, too."

"She's out," Dustin told him. "She's in the ambulance, where you should be."

"Oh, thank God." The man surged to his feet, grabbing Brooke's hand, his eyes wet. "I'm sorry. I'm so sorry—"

She shook her head. "You need to sit down—"

"No, I'm fine. I'm just so damn sorry—"

Dustin brought him to Claire, while Brooke stared up at the building, which was a virtual inferno.

Zach was in there.

She took a step toward it but Dustin was back, blocking her path. *"What are you doing?"*

"I need to get closer."

"You're not a firefighter. And we're hospital-bound, Brooke. Two vics, remember? It's our job."

Damn it, he was right. The job. The job always came first. It was what she'd signed on for, and she'd never before minded it taking over her life. Not once.

Unfortunately, she'd given herself a taste of *real* life here in Santa Rey, and she liked it. Hell, loved it.

But now the person who'd given her that taste of life was in danger of losing his.

BROOKE AND DUSTIN were still unloading their patients at the E.R. when word came from the fire scene that they had the flames eighty percent contained, and the injured firefighters had been evacuated safely.

Alive.

And on the way to the hospital.

Brooke took her first deep breath since she'd heard the words *firefighters* and *down* in the same sentence. She and Dustin tried to wait but an emergency call came in for them—a woman with chest pains needed assistance.

While Dustin drove, Brooke called Aidan.

"Blake's in surgery," Aidan said, sounding tense and stressed. "Badly broken leg."

Ohmigod. "Zach?"

"A concussion, broken wrist and a few second-degree burns. I know that sounds bad, but he's going to be okay, Brooke."

Relief hit her like a tidal wave, but she couldn't lose it because they'd arrived at their call, where she and Dustin found a three-hundred-and-fifty-pound woman stuck in her bed, needing assistance to the bathroom.

"You said you had chest pains," Dustin said.

"Right. I do. But I think it's heartburn."

"Are the pains gone now?" Brooke asked.

"Yes. Completely."

"Ma'am, we still need to bring you in to be checked—"

"Okay, so I never had chest pains. I called because you people won't come out unless it's serious."

They were speechless.

"Would you hand me my TV remote?" she asked them. "Oh, and that box of doughnuts?"

Brooke stared at her. She'd missed being at Zach's side for this, for a woman who couldn't reach her damn remote so she'd called 911? She handed over the remote but not the doughnuts. "Ma'am, the 911 system is for *real* emergencies—"

"It was a real emergency."

Dustin still couldn't speak.

"Hey, I'm sorry, but *Grey's Anatomy* is repeating and I missed it the first time around."

"*Medical* emergencies," Brooke said tightly.

The woman finally had the grace to look a little abashed. "I know, but who else am I going to call?"

"You could do it yourself." No longer speechless, Dustin was clearly furious. "Consider it your daily exercise."

They left there in silence, and it was several long moments before either could speak.

"That didn't just happen," Dustin finally said.

But unfortunately it had, and they had another call, and then another, and it was several hours before Brooke could get another status check on Zach. By that time he'd been released from the hospital and was at his house, supposedly resting.

She wanted to get over there, needed to get a good look at him herself and make sure he was okay, but the chief put their rig on overtime; neither she nor Dustin was going anywhere.

It killed her.

She'd always given her heart and soul to her job, and that had always fulfilled her. But she could see that was no longer the case. Zach's accident had driven home to her that work was *not* enough.

Here in Santa Rey, she'd found more.

14

WHEN THE DOORBELL rang late that night, Zach was in bed, nicely doped up, flying high on whatever the doctor had given him. Aidan had already brought him dinner and had stayed for a movie, but was gone now. Jenny had brought another movie and a few of her pole-dancing pals by, but they'd left, too.

And now someone else was ringing… He sat up very carefully, and then stayed there, head spinning. He'd never been injured on the job before and wasn't quite sure how it had happened. He remembered nearly getting outside the burning building, but that was all until he'd woken up to a headache from hell and Aidan pulling his sorry ass out of the fire just before it ate them both alive.

He knew the dangers of his job. Hell, he knew the dangers of life, but that reality hadn't hit him since his parents had died.

It hit him now. He could have died.

Morbid thought, but he was a realist. If he'd died, life would go on. People would mourn, sure, but no one's basic existence would change with his passing, and that meant facing something uncomfortable—he hadn't made much of a dent.

After his parents' death, he'd just gone along, minding

his business, working hard, playing even harder, and that had always been enough for him, because why go for more when life was so damn short? He'd always looked at his colleagues, the ones who'd tied themselves down with marriages and kids, and had been thankful it wasn't him.

But now he couldn't help but wonder if he'd missed out on something that he'd never fathomed.

The doorbell rang again.

"Coming!" he called out, then instantly regretted it because that hurt. Note to self: *don't yell.* Getting out of bed wasn't too much of a problem, but remaining upright proved to be. It turned out his head didn't feel quite attached, and he brought up his uncasted wrist to hold it in place as he made his way to the door like someone on a three-day drunk. He managed to unlock it, then sagged back against the wall, weary to his bones of the jackhammer going off inside his skull. Everything hurt—his wrist, the burns on his left shoulder, arm and chest…

The door creaked open. "Zach?"

Ah, he knew that voice. He knew what it sounded like when she was in the throes of an orgasm, panting, sobbing for breath. He knew what it sounded like when she was slowly drifting back to him, and his name rolled off her tongue as if maybe, just maybe, he were the best she'd ever had.

At the sight of him, she let out a little gasp. "Zach, you shouldn't be up."

"You rang."

"Oh, God. I'm sorry." And then her hands were on his waist, gently pulling him away from the wall so she could slip her shoulder beneath his good one and wrap an arm around him, supporting his weight. "Okay?" she asked.

He slung his arm around her and smiled into her face. "Okay." She was wearing a tank top and capris, looking as if she was learning to fit into the beach world after all. Her hair had been pulled back as usual, neat and tidy as could be, so he tugged on her ponytail, just enough to have some strands slipping free. "There," he said. "A little messy. I like you that way best."

"Bed," she said firmly.

"I thought you'd never ask."

She gave him a look. "What do they have you on?"

"Good stuff."

"Sounds like it." One arm was firmly around him, the other hand low on his abs. He wouldn't have thought it possible, but she was actually completely supporting him, even though he was a foot taller and probably had seventy pounds on her.

As he'd always known, the little city girl was a helluva lot tougher than she looked.

At the top of the stairs, she kept moving to his bedroom. He was just dizzy and shaken enough to let her put him to bed, although he did attempt to pull her down with him. "You need liquids," she said. "Water? Tea?"

"A kiss."

"Both," she decided, and vanished.

Uptight, stubborn as a mule, know-it-all, anal woman.

When she came back and set a tray on his nightstand, he struggled to open his eyes, surprised to find even that took effort. "I'm cold," he said. "Possibly hypothermic."

"I'll get you a blanket."

"You're supposed to offer to strip down and press

your heated body to mine. It's in all the movies. The girl always strips."

"Zach." With her hands on her hips, and her hair suitably messed up thanks to his doing, Brooke looked so pretty and sexy he couldn't think straight.

And she had no idea. No idea at all that she messed with his head just by being. "You really should be out by now," he said, bemused.

"I'm not leaving you alone."

"I meant out of my head." He closed his eyes. "I can't get you out of my damn head."

What if *she'd* gotten hurt today? What if *she'd* died? At the thought, his throat closed up. Just refused to suck air into his lungs, because apparently he'd screwed up and let himself care. If something ever happened to her...

He'd never put words to his biggest fear before, but he was doing so now. And he didn't like it. Not at all.

"Zach." Softly, gently, she cupped his face. "You're in my head, too. *Way* too much."

He hadn't planned to go there—had, in fact, never planned to go there again. His parents dying had nearly been the end of him. "It's the drugs for me." He closed his eyes. "What's your excuse?"

She was quiet a moment. "Maybe you've proven irresistible."

He tried to laugh, but that hurt, so he sobered up quickly. "If it'd been you..."

"But it wasn't. I'm fine." She stretched out next to him on his bed and gently pressed her body to his aching one, easing his pain with no effort at all.

With a sigh, he pulled her closer, holding her tight, tucking her head beneath his chin, wondering how it was that suddenly, with her here in his arms, everything felt all right.

"Are you really okay?" she whispered. Pulling back, she looked up into his face. Her eyes were bright, and warm, and so open Zach could see into her soul.

Was he okay? He didn't feel it. Things had gotten a little crazy in that fire—maybe it was just residual adrenaline making him need her so. "If I said I'm not okay, what would you do?"

Her fingers drifted over his chest in a touch he knew she meant to be soothing, but was actually having an entirely different effect. "I'd do everything in my power to make you comfortable."

"Then, no." He went to shake his head, but the pain stopped him cold. "Definitely not okay."

"Tell me what hurts."

He looked deep into her eyes and saw so much. So much that he had to close his own.

Coward. Yeah, despite the tough-guy image his job gave him, he was a coward. At least he knew it, knew his limitations, knew that loving her, loving anyone, was something he couldn't do. "What hurts?" He stayed very still. "Everything hurts like hell."

Leaning over him, she very carefully kissed his jaw beneath a bruise. "Does that help?"

"Yeah," he decided. "Yeah, definitely."

"How about here…" She kissed him again, closer to his ear this time, making his breath catch.

"Uh-huh."

"Maybe I should kiss all your hurts."

"Okay."

"Tell me where," she murmured.

"Here." He pointed to his throat.

Nodding somberly but with a hint of humor in her beautiful eyes, she obediently kissed his throat, slowly, hotly, with a touch of tongue that shot all the blood in his head to his groin in zero point four.

"Where else?" she asked against his skin, her hand slipping down his side, then back up again, lifting his T-shirt as she went. "Here?" She kissed him over the bandage on his left shoulder and part of his chest, and then the other side, where there were no bandages, just skin, and he felt his heart leap. "Zach?"

"Yeah, there—" He broke off on a shaky breath when she licked his nipple and then began a trail of hot, wet, openmouthed kisses down his torso, southbound.

"Maybe here, too?" She was at his abs now, her fingers toying with the string tie of his sweats. She stopped to glance up at him with an expression that said there was nowhere on earth she'd rather be than right here licking him.

He could come from just looking at her. "Everywhere," he said hoarsely, and felt her yank on the tie and slip her hand inside, beneath the material, wrapping those magic fingers around him. "God, Brooke."

"Shh." She worked his sweats down. "I'm healing you here." Her lips hovered over him and he held his breath, which came out in a rush when she kissed him.

And then drew him gently into her mouth. He lost himself for a while after that, but managed to tug her up before he exploded. "Skin to skin," he whispered, and with an eager smile, she pulled off her clothes, and then with such slow care that he was aching by the end of it, she removed the rest of his, as well, before raiding his nightstand for a condom. Shaking with need, he pulled her down over the tip of him and kissed her as she spread her legs, straddling his, and brought him home.

Sensations swamped him, but then she began to move so that he slid in and out of her, in and out, and he lost his breath again. Time drifted away, his entire world shrinking down to the feel of her surrounding him, milking him, and he had to fight the inclination of his own body to let go and fly.

"Are you hurting?" she murmured, her mouth on his jaw, her hands—just her hands had him letting out a groan of agonized pleasure. "Zach?" She stilled. "Am I hurting you?"

"*Killing* me." He swept his one good hand down her back to grip her sweet, sweet ass, loving the way she panted his name softly in his ear. Slipping his fingers in her silky wet heat, he stroked and teased, doing his damnedest to bring her up to speed to where he was, which was standing on the edge, teetering, so desperate for the plunge he shook with it.

"Zach—"

Unable to help it, he thrust up into her. She was letting out soft whimpers with every breath, assuring him she was as turned on as he.

"Zach, I'm going to—"

"Do it. Come," he murmured against her mouth. "I want to feel you."

And she did. She came completely undone for him, on him, her unbound hair in his face, her fingers tightening painfully in his hair. She was breathless, crying out, and he was gasping as her tightening thighs and the slow grind of her hips set off his own climax. He followed her over, swamped with a tidal wave of unnamed emotion as he poured himself into her.

A WHISPER, then a low male laugh broke through Brooke's subconscious, and then it all came back to her. Going to Zach's house, him answering the door, her taking in all that rumpled, surfer-boy glory.

Taking him to bed, taking him *on* the bed, seeing the look in his eyes that told her he was way more invested in her than he wanted to believe or admit…

She opened her eyes. Yep, still in bed with Zach. Actually, she was wrapped around him like a pretzel, thankfully with the covers up to their chin, because at the foot of the bed stood Aidan, Sam, Cristina and Dustin.

"Definitely, he's doing better than Blake," Dustin said. "Blake didn't have a woman with him in his hospital bed."

They were holding fast-food bags, and, as Sam so cheerfully held up to reveal, porn. "To cheer you up."

"But apparently Brooke had other ideas on how to cheer him up," Cristina said.

Dustin shushed her.

"Well, she did." Cristina gave him a little shove. "And as I told *you* before you turned me down, sex is really good for cheering people up."

Everyone looked at Dustin, who shifted uncomfortably. "Maybe I don't like casual cheer-up sex," he said in self-defense.

"Everyone likes casual cheer-up sex," Cristina scoffed. "*Normal* people like casual cheer-up sex."

"Maybe I like it to mean something." Dustin looked into her eyes. "Maybe I want to know it's going to happen again."

She jabbed him in the pec with a finger. "I told you, I don't make plans."

Dustin lifted a shoulder, wordlessly admitting they were at an impasse.

Cristina glared at him, then at the others. "And what are you all looking at?"

In unison, eyes swiveled away from the train wreck waiting to happen, to the other train wreck that had already happened.

Brooke, in Zach's arms.

In his bed.

Surrounded by goggling eyes.

"Get out," Zach said to them all. "And Aidan, I want my key back."

"You gave it to me for emergencies."

"Is there an emergency?"

"Well, I thought junk food and porn constituted one, but I can see I was mistaken."

"Brooke's hair is down," Sam noted. "That's new."

"Out." Zach pointed at the bedroom door with his injured arm. *"Now."*

When they'd filed out, Brooke covered her face. "This is bad. I fell asleep—"

"It's okay."

"They thought it was funny!"

"It is funny," he said. "A little."

Slipping out of the bed, she hurriedly reached for her clothes. Hearing the guys in the kitchen, digging into the food, she felt naked.

Very, very naked. "I've got to go."

"At least stay and eat."

She couldn't stay. Not right now. Not when she'd just

realized that in her heart, she was like Dustin, and not cut out for this lightweight sex thing. In spite of herself and her promise on that night on that rock, her damn heart had opened to Zach.

How stupid was that? She'd fallen all the way, leaving herself vulnerable to pain. And there would be pain. She was okay with that, but she needed a moment, a few moments, before she could smile and mean it.

"Hey. *Hey,*" he said when she turned away, snagging her hand, pulling her back. "Brooke? What is it?" The bruise on his jaw had darkened, the white bandage wrapped around his left shoulder stark against his tanned skin. He had bed-head again, and tired eyes that said he was hurting like hell.

He didn't need this, the burden of her feelings. "I need to go home for clothes before work," she said, faking a smile. "That's all."

He was quiet while she pulled on her shirt, so quiet that she finally glanced over to find him looking at her. And in his eyes was a wariness because he felt things for her, too, she knew he did, feelings he kept inside because he didn't intend to let them go anywhere—but what was worse was the comprehension she found there.

Oh, God. Despite her best effort, he could see what she was feeling. "Yeah, I really, *really* have to go."

With a wince, he sat up in bed. "Brooke—"

"No." She shook her head. "Please don't say anything."

"I'm sorry."

Oh, God. "Don't be silly. You have nothing to be sorry for."

"Yes, I do. I'm sorry that I can't give you what you want."

Casually as she could, she slipped into her shoes and attempted to wrangle her hair. "And what is it you think I want?"

Reaching out, he grabbed her hand again, stilling her frenetic movements, waiting until she looked at him. "Love," he said quietly.

She managed a light laugh. She realized she might be pathetically needy when it came to that particular emotion, but love hadn't exactly been prominent in her life. She'd come here to Santa Rey a little bit in limbo, but the one thing she'd known was she'd wanted that to change. But she'd made Zach a promise *not* to get attached, *not* to have messy emotions.

She'd failed on both counts.

"Brooke." He stroked a strand of hair from her face, all the while holding her gaze with his so that she couldn't look away to save her life. In these eyes were affection, heat…and a brutal honesty. "I don't want to hurt you. I never wanted to hurt you, but—"

"It's not your fault—"

"I wanted a physical relationship with you, you know that. And now I'm holding back, you know that, too. It's just that if you're going to add love into the mix—" He grinned ruefully. "Well, you can't. I don't seem to have the parts required to do love. So you can't fall, not for me."

Her throat tight, she nodded. "I know."

Only she also knew it was too damn late.

15

ZACH SLEPT on and off for two days. Or rather he tossed and turned for two days. He spent his third night at home surrounded by the guys, grateful not to still be in the hospital like Blake, who'd suffered a more serious head trauma, his leg broken in four places, and two cracked ribs, and was by all accounts cranky as all hell.

Zach was glad for the company. Sort of. But mostly he kept thinking about the fact that Brooke hadn't come back, and that this was her last week in town, and that he was an idiot.

"Why are you moping around like you lost your puppy?" Sam asked.

"I'm not."

The guys all exchanged a careful-with-the-deluded-patient look, and he sighed.

Yeah. He was moping.

Because he'd sent away the best thing that had ever happened to him.

"You've got pizza, beer and us," Eddie joked. "What else could you need?"

"Brooke." This from Aidan, his mouth full of pizza and a knowing look in his eyes. "He wants Brooke."

"No." Sam shook his head. "Our Zach's not much of a repeater."

Zach opened his mouth, but in lieu of absolutely nothing to say in his defense, shut it again.

"If I had Brooke looking at me the way she looks at you, I'd become a repeater," Dustin said as he reached for more pizza.

Yeah, but Zach was a moron. Brooke wouldn't be looking at him like that again. He'd made sure of that.

"You're only saying so because you got laid by the woman of your dreams," Sam pointed out. "Cristina."

"Cristina?" Zach blinked. This was news. "Since when?"

"Since last night," Sam informed him. "Dustin fixed her car and then she slept with him."

Not one to kiss and tell, Dustin tried to hold back his stupid grin and failed.

"Cristina's not going to settle down," Aidan warned Dustin. "She's not the type."

"She might, for the right guy," Dustin said, pushing up his glasses. "It could happen."

"You're asking to be crushed," Aidan told him. "Like a grape. *Again.*"

"Actually," Zach said quietly, "you never know."

"Then why aren't you seeing Brooke?" Aidan asked. "With only one week in town left, that makes her the perfect woman in my eyes."

"So why don't *you* date her?" Eddie jeered.

"Maybe I will."

Suddenly the pizza Zach had consumed sat like a lead weight in his gut. He tried to picture Brooke moving on and dating any one of these guys. His friends.

Then he had to admit it wasn't the pizza weighing his gut down. "No."

Aidan raised a brow. "What?"

"Nothing." Zach tossed his pizza aside. "She can date whoever she wants."

"Really?" Aidan said dryly. "So you wouldn't care if I ask her out?"

Zach opened his mouth, shut it, scrubbed a hand over his eyes and sighed. "We've been friends for a long time."

"Years."

"Yeah. And I've always said you should go out with whoever floats your boat, but…"

"But?"

"But if you go out with Brooke, I'll have to hurt you."

Dustin laughed and clamped him on the shoulder in commiseration.

Aidan just arched a brow that said, *You're in deep.*

Didn't he know it.

LATER THAT DAY, the bad news came from Zach's doctor—he wasn't cleared to go back to work until his cast came off, which was a minimum of three weeks away.

Three more weeks without work just might kill him, not that the doctor seemed to care, and not that the chief seemed to, either, when he called to check on Zach.

"Enjoy the time off. We'll be waiting for you."

"I want to come in," Zach said. "I could handle light duty—"

"No. We want you back, Zach, but sound."

Sound. What the hell did that mean?

But as the mind-numbing boredom set in, Zach had to admit he didn't feel so *sound.* He sat on his couch with the remote, but nothing on daytime TV interested him.

Nothing on his bookshelf interested him. Hell, even the porn didn't interest him. He couldn't go surfing because of the cast and bandages. He couldn't work.

All he could do, unfortunately, was think. *Way* too much thinking going on. About Brooke, about… Brooke.

It was another whole day before he remembered.

The arson fires. He'd actually come close to figuring something out…something really important. He called Aidan. "Where was I with the arson stuff?"

"Close to screwing up your career."

"Come on. We've fought hundreds of fires, and out of all of those, I'm only talking about four—"

"Five."

"—So how in the hell is that screwing up my career—"

"Five fires."

"What?"

Aidan sighed. "Let's get real crazy, okay? I think that the warehouse fire was arson."

"Why?"

"Gut feeling. Too many things went wrong. And guess what Tommy told me when I mentioned it?"

"I'll go out on a limb here and say, 'Mind your own fucking business?'"

"Bingo."

"Did you look around afterward?" Zach asked. "Get sight of the point of origin?"

"No, I was sitting by your side in the hospital after saving your sorry ass."

"Damn it."

"You're welcome."

After they hung up, Zach went out onto his deck and

stared off into the night. Maybe it was exhaustion, maybe it was pain, maybe it was simply that he didn't want to face the fact that his chest hurt, and so did his heart.

Or that he missed Brooke.

Over the years, he'd slept with enough women to lose count, and that had never bothered him any, but now he wondered what it would be like to stay with the *same* woman instead of moving on each time? To have some familiarity? A real relationship with depth instead of just heat?

He bet there was comfort in that, which he'd never had any use for before. But now, honestly, he could use a little TLC.

Zach hadn't taken his pain meds in two days, so showering was a bitch, but he got through it, dressed and walked out to his truck. He stopped short at the sight of Brooke getting out of her car.

She was carrying a bag from the local sandwich shop and wore an expression that said she wasn't too sure of her welcome, an expression that changed to disbelief when she saw the keys in his hand. "What are you doing?"

"I was going to ask you the same thing."

"I'm bringing you something more substantial than pizza or McDonald's." Her eyes met his. "Now you."

"I was coming to see you."

She let out a breath. "Okay, you have no idea how I both love and hate that. You shouldn't be driving. How are you feeling?"

Like I missed the hell out of you. "Great."

She arched a brow.

"Good."

"Zach."

"Okay, like shit. I feel like complete shit."

With a sigh, she stepped close, and did something he hadn't expected, given how things had gone the last time he'd seen her.

She hugged him.

For a moment, just a heartbeat, really, he stood still, shocked, because normally when he pushed someone away, they willingly went. After all, he was a master pusher when it came right down to it. And he'd all but thrown her feelings for him back in her face.

But Brooke, petite, sweet-but-steely-willed Brooke, hadn't just held her ground with him, she was pushing back.

If that didn't grab him by the throat.

Unable to resist, he slid his arms around her, pulling her in tight. Bending his head, he buried his face in her hair, breathing her in.

Keep it light, keep it casual…

But then she was pressing her mouth to his cheek and he was turning his head to meet her mouth, and as he deepened the kiss he knew the truth.

He didn't want to push her away anymore. He really didn't. So he hoped like hell someone threw him a line, because he was going down.

"You need to get back inside," she murmured. "You're pale."

Pale, and apparently stupid, because he kissed her again. Deep.

Wet.

He was in the middle of working on the long part, but she pulled back. "Careful, I'll hurt you—"

Shaking his head, he kissed her again, then dropped

his forehead to hers. "No." Drawing a deep breath, he straightened and pulled free. "I'll hurt you."

"Oh." She stared up at him, then took a step back and nodded. "Right."

They were still just staring at each other when Aidan pulled up, followed by all the guys.

Incredible timing, as always.

"Okay," Brooke said. "I'm going to go."

"No, don't."

"No, really. It's okay. I just wanted—" She thrust the bag of food in his hands. "Here."

"Wait—"

"Listen, I know I wear my heart on my sleeve and feel too much, but I'm not slow. I really did hear you the other day, what you were trying to say. You don't want me to get invested, and I get it. I'm leaving and all that, and this was never about that kind of thing. I just want you to know that I understand, and there's no hard feelings."

Damn, she killed him. "Brooke—"

"Don't." She shook her head. "Don't go there. Not now."

"Fine. Later, then. Just please stay until I get rid of these guys?"

She glanced at them all getting out of their cars. "Okay, but Zach? That kiss…"

He couldn't help looking at her lips again. He could still taste her. "Yeah?"

"That didn't feel like a hey-how-are-you kiss. Or even a one-night-stand kiss." She moved in and whispered for his ears only. "It felt like a helluva lot more."

Yeah. It had.

"So you might want to think about that next time you tell yourself I'm the only one going to get hurt here."

EVERYONE ENTERED Zach's house, carrying food and news of their day. Brooke joined them because Zach had asked, but mostly because she wanted to. She wanted to be with them.

With Zach.

He sat sprawled on the couch, and if it hadn't been for the cast, the bandages and the slight paleness of his face, she'd never have guessed that he'd nearly died.

Her heart tightened at that, but she'd always licked her wounds in private, so stressing about what could have happened, as she had been doing since the fire, would have to wait.

Sam tossed her a soda.

Dustin handed her a plate.

Aidan kicked a chair her way.

She sat in the chair, holding the soda and plate, staring at the group talking and laughing amongst themselves, a huge lump forming in her throat.

She really was part of them. She belonged. And hadn't that been what she'd been looking for at the beginning of the summer? A place to belong?

Zach sipped his soda, his eyes hooded as he watched her over his drink.

She watched him back.

Around them, the laughter and noise went up a notch, but Zach didn't join in. Probably because he was hurting far more than he'd let on. She could see it in the grim set of his mouth and the lines of exhaustion on his face. He eyed the pizza on the coffee table in front of him but didn't take a piece.

He loved pizza.

"You okay?" Aidan leaned in to ask her quietly.

"Not me I'm worried about."

They both eyed Zach. "Let's try this." Aidan tossed two slices of pieces on a plate, then handed it to Zach. "Hey. The annual picnic is in one week."

"So?"

"So we need an anchor for the tug-of-war against Firehouse 32."

"I repeat. So?"

"So no pansy-asses need apply. Eat up."

"Not hungry."

"Really? You like being home all day, watching *Oprah,* eating bonbons?"

Zach opened his mouth, probably to tell Aidan where to go, but the doorbell rang again, and in came Cristina, carrying a tray of cupcakes.

Everyone looked at Dustin. Everyone except Cristina, that is, alerting Brooke to the fact that something was going on. Happy not to be at the center of the gossip mill for once, she watched with fascination as the blonde shuffled around without her usual cockiness.

"The grocery store had a small fire in their bakery." She set the tray down and grabbed a cupcake in each hand before looking at the gang, carefully avoiding Dustin's eyes. "So, what's up?"

"Nothing," everyone but Dustin said.

Cristina sighed and faced the silent and clearly brooding Dustin. "Okay, fine. I'm sorry." She offered him a cupcake. "Very sorry."

Dustin stared down at the double chocolate fudge cupcake, eyes shadowed, mouth unaccustomedly tight. He didn't take it. "What's this?"

"It's called dessert. It's what people do when they're sorry. They bring people treats."

"Why are you sorry?"

"You know why."

"Say I don't."

Cristina sighed. "I'm sorry I got mad when you wouldn't have sex with me again."

Dustin raised a brow in tune to the juvenile catcalls from the guys.

"I *am* sorry, all right?" Cristina ignored everyone else. "Jesus! Would you just eat a damn cupcake?"

"I don't think so."

"Oh my God." Cristina sighed again, looking at the others, all of whom got real busy with their cupcakes. "Look, I really needed to get laid, okay? It'd been too long and you might have noticed that I was a little on edge."

"Was?"

She rolled her eyes.

"Maybe you're on edge for other reasons," Dustin said. "Ever think of that?"

"No." She waggled the cupcake in front of his nose. "Are you going to take this or not?"

Dustin took it, then licked the frosting while studying Cristina thoughtfully.

The room was unusually quiet now. Brooke was especially so, mostly because she really felt for Dustin. He'd put himself out there and was now hurting.

She knew the feeling.

"I'm sorry, too," Dustin said, mouth full of frosting.

Cristina went still. "For?"

"For not having more meaningless sex with you."

Sam let out a choked laugh and, without taking her eyes off Dustin, Cristina pointed at him.

Sam shut up.

"Does that mean you want to?" Cristina asked Dustin. "Have more meaningless sex?"

"No."

Cristina looked deeply disappointed, but tried to hide it. "Okay."

"*I'll* have meaningless sex with you," Eddie said. When Cristina rounded on him, Aidan helpfully stuffed a cupcake into Eddie's mouth to keep him quiet.

"Or you could try it my way," Dustin suggested to Cristina.

Cristina turned back to Dustin and blinked.

Dustin didn't.

Zach sighed, and with some struggle, stood up, gesturing the others to follow him, clearly not wanting to stay and witness the bloodshed.

This time, Cristina pointed at Zach. "Don't move. Did you put him up to this?"

"Give me some credit," Dustin answered for him. "I've had it bad for you since day one. There's no way you haven't noticed."

"Whoa." Cristina staggered back a step and collided with a wall. "What? What the hell did you just say?"

"I gave you an offer for sex," Dustin said calmly. "As I believe you were lamenting about your continued lack of."

"After that," she whispered.

"I said give me some credit. Of course Zach didn't put me up to this."

"No, after that." She swallowed hard. *"What the hell did you say after that?"*

"The part where I said I've wanted you since day one?"

"Yeah. Hang on." And she sat, right there on the floor. "That."

With a sigh, Dustin got up and crouched in front of her. "It's not a death sentence, Cristina."

"Ohmigod."

He sighed again. "I was hoping for a more articulate response than that."

"Articulate?" She looked bowled over, but he just waited, and she swallowed hard. "Okay, articulate. How about…" She shook her head as if at a loss. "Thank you?"

He arched a brow. "Thank you?"

"Look, I'm trying to be polite here, but I really need to throw up. Are you crazy? You've got a thing for me? You don't even know all my faults."

"I think I know a lot of them," he said dryly.

"Ohmigod."

"You're starting to repeat yourself. Let's go for a walk."

"A walk."

"Yes. On the beach."

"Are you trying to romance me?"

"Uh-huh. Is it working?"

"I don't know. Maybe. No more talk about…wanting me. Promise?"

"Take my hand, Cristina."

She stared at his proffered hand, and then took it. "You should know I'm not putting out on the first date."

"Maybe on our second, then."

That shook a laugh out of her and, shocking Brooke and probably everyone else, Cristina allowed Dustin to pull her out the door.

Brooke watched them go, something deep inside her aching. Then she realized Zach was looking right at her. What she'd give to know that he was aching, too, but whatever he was thinking, he kept it to himself.

A LITTLE WHILE LATER, Zach managed to escape to the kitchen, where he leaned on the sink and stared out the window. He could still hear his friends talking and laughing in the other room. He was grateful for them, but he wished they'd all go away and leave him alone with Brooke.

The door opened and he turned hopefully, but it was Tommy.

"How are you feeling?" the inspector asked.

"I'd be better if you'd convince the chief to let me go back to work."

"No can do."

"Tommy—"

He held up a hand. "I agree with you about those fires," he said quietly. "Okay? You're right. They're arson, all of them. I've always believed you." He let that sink in. "But believing you wasn't the problem. My investigation was—is—undercover."

Zach stared at him. "Because…you suspected me."

Tommy's expression was apologetic but firm. "Past tense."

Zach let out a breath. "Jesus, Tommy."

"I know you want to come back to work, but I'm advising you to wait."

"You don't think—"

"What I think is that you're in danger."

"What the hell does that mean?"

"You've been a damn thorn for me, Zach, and we're

on the same side. Imagine how the bad guy feels about you."

"I don't understand."

"You're getting close. Close enough for the arsonist to try to hurt you. He burned Phyllis's house because you care about her. Then at the warehouse fire, you were hit."

"By a burning piece of ceiling."

"By a chunk of debris, yes, but I've been at the site. I think it was thrown at you."

Zach staggered to a chair and sat.

"I've combed every inch of that site," Tommy said. "You went back in where you weren't supposed to, and I believe you almost caught the arsonist red-handed."

"But the only people inside at that point, besides the victims, were firefighters."

Tommy just looked at him, and that's when he finally got it. They weren't looking for some nameless criminal.

It was someone they all knew.

16

AFTER EVERYONE had gone, Brooke grabbed a trash bag and started to clean up.

"Leave it," Zach told her, weary to the bone. "I can do it."

She put her hands on her hips. "You're going to do it?"

"Yes."

"Even though you've barely moved all night?"

He lifted a shoulder, which pulled at his burns and had pain shooting through him. He didn't make a sound, he very carefully didn't make a sound, but she was at his side in a heartbeat.

"Damn stubborn man," she murmured, helping him up.

Suddenly, all he could think about was how her hands felt on him. "What are you doing?"

"Putting you to bed."

Just the words had his body leaping to attention. Even in pain and pissed off at the world, he could still get it up for her. "Sorry, but I'm bound to disappoint you tonight."

"Shut up, Zach."

Upstairs in his room, she got him onto the bed. He looked up into her face. Her beautiful face. She was worried sick, and, he realized with some shame, that he was not the only one hurting. "I talked to Tommy tonight. He said he believed me."

"What?" Brooke went still. "Oh, Zach," she breathed. "I'm so glad! Does he know who the arsonist is?"

This was the hard part. "He suspects an inside job."

"Inside…" Her mind worked fast, and she gasped. "No."

"The warehouse fire wasn't an accident." He went to reach for her and gritted his teeth at the pain.

"I'm going to get your meds and water. Don't move."

When she was gone, he tried to pull off his shoes, but the cast on his arm felt heavy. Plus, moving hurt. Not feeling up to taking off his own damn shirt, much less his pants, he lay back on the bed, out of breath and frustrated.

"Why don't you get undressed?" she asked, coming back into the room with a glass of water and a pill.

He closed his eyes. "Yeah. Good idea."

"Need help?"

"No. I can do this. Seriously."

"Seriously? Get real, Zach." He felt her hands pulling off his shoes, heard them hit the floor one at a time. "Because, seriously? You are full of shit." Carefully, with a surprisingly gentle touch considering the sarcasm in her voice, she helped him out of his shirt. "So what else did Tommy say?"

"That I've pissed off the arsonist."

She went still. "You're in danger?"

"I'm safe here."

Her eyes searched his as her hands slid over his bare chest.

Instead of the pain he'd felt for days, all he felt was the touch of her warm hands. She was better than Vicodin. Then she trailed those hands down and reached for the buttons on his Levi's. "You still need my help, right?"

Oh, yeah. He nodded, and pop went the first button. And then the second, and suddenly Zach was breathing as if he'd been running.

She wasn't breathing too steadily, either.

"Okay, maybe I'd better do this." His hands were shaking as he pulled open the rest of the buttons, but shoving the denim down his legs required grating his teeth and lifting his hips. By the time he got them down a mere inch, he was beginning to sweat.

"Here." She got on the bed for leverage, straddling his lower legs, and pulled his jeans down to his thighs, revealing the fact that he'd gone commando that morning.

Which left the part of him that was the happiest to see her bouncing free.

Her eyes widened.

"I told you I should do this."

"I'm sorry." She was still staring.

"Not helping."

At that, Brooke actually snickered, but he could hear the breathlessness in the sound.

And the wanting.

"Yeah," he managed. "Still not helping."

"Right." She scrambled off his legs.

Good. Great. She was going away. But then she pulled his jeans the rest of the way off, tossing them to the floor. Leaving him buck naked.

"You…need a blanket."

Which was beneath him. He rolled toward her just as she leaned in to try to pull it out from under him, and they bumped into each other.

"Sorry," she gasped, but in countering her own movement, she bumped into him again.

They went utterly still.

He had his hands on her arms. She had hers braced on his chest, and she was still staring at the part of him boring a hold in her belly.

"Zach?" she whispered.

"Yeah?"

"You seem to need some…" Her gaze met his. "Letting loose."

He laughed, which hurt like a son of a bitch.

"Yeah?"

"Oh, yeah. It's just what I need." *You…* And with that, he tugged her overtop of him.

AT THE FULL BODY CONTACT with Zach, what happened within Brooke was what happened every time—a shockingly intense, insatiable hunger arose. "Zach—"

"I know. Condom."

She leaned over and grabbed one from his nightstand, while he tugged at her zipper, but his fingers were shaking. "Why are you wearing so many clothes?"

"I have no idea—" Before she got the words out, Zach had her capris down and pushed open her legs. Pretty damn talented for a man with one arm. Then he lifted her up and thrust into her.

Their twin groans of pleasure mingled in the air.

Her hands were braced on either side of his face, her head bent low to his. Staring into his eyes, she was startled at how easily she lost herself in him.

Every.

Single.

Time.

Brooke had no idea how she could want him this way,

as if she would die if she didn't have him. The hunger filled her so that she could think of nothing else, and she rocked her hips, a movement that wrested a grunt from him. His good hand gripped her, holding her still. "Don't move." His voice was like sandpaper. "God, don't move, or this'll be over—"

She moved. She couldn't help it; she had to. She rocked her hips again, absorbing the low, rough sound torn from deep in his throat. Leaning over him, she went to bury her face in the crook of his neck but he caught her, cupped her jaw and held it so that she could do nothing but look right into his eyes as he met her thrust for thrust, until she began to tremble, then burst. He was right with her, pulsing inside her even as she shattered around him.

"Yeah." He breathed a shaky sigh as she sagged over top of him, a boneless puddle of raw nerve endings. "Just what the doctor ordered." She felt his mouth press to the side of her throat and closed her eyes, letting the drowsiness take her—which was infinitely preferable to facing the fact that she had no idea how she was going to walk away from this man.

BROOKE AWOKE to the sun pouring in through the window and splashing all over her face with startling cheer.

But she always shut her shades, so…

She jerked upright. Yep, she wasn't in her bed, she was in Zach's. Legs entwined, arms entwined, no covers in sight because their body heat had been enough. Once again she'd slept the entire night wrapped around him as if…

As if she belonged here.

Zach stirred, opened an eye. He had two days' growth on his jaw, and some serious bed-head, and he looked so hot she wanted to gobble him up.

Again.

"Overslept," she said, and tried to free herself. "Going to be late—" She broke off when he merely tightened his grip on her. "What?"

"Just wondering if it worked. If I'm suitably relaxed or if maybe we should kept working on it."

She stared into his gorgeous, sleepy face and remembered his warning not to fall in love with him. "You're fine." She scrambled up, glanced at the clock again on the off chance it had miraculously changed in her favor. "Where the hell are my panties?"

Zach came up on an elbow and surveyed the room. "There."

On his lamp. Perfect. Her bra was draped over a bedpost like a trophy. Snatching it up, she glared at him, just lying there looking like sin on a stick. "I'm late," she said more to herself. Very late. Late for the rest of her life, which was right around the corner. In fact, she was meeting the real estate agent today to discuss an offer she'd received on the house yesterday. With a sigh, she headed toward the door.

"Brooke?"

She turned back. "Yes?"

"Be careful out there."

"I always am."

"I know. But…"

But now one of them was a possible arsonist and had hurt Zach. Anyone could get hurt. She got that. "I can take care of myself."

"But—"

"And after next week, I'll be on my own." Because that brought a lump to her throat, she had to swallow hard to continue. "I realize that last night was mostly my doing, but you should know, I got an offer on the house. Three more shifts, and I'm gone."

He closed his eyes, but not before she saw a flash of emotion much deeper than affection. "I know."

"Goodbye, Zach."

Now he opened those eyes again, and let her see his sadness. "Is that it? Goodbye, the end?"

"What else is there?"

When he opened his mouth and then shut it, she shook her head. "Exactly. Goodbye, Zach."

WELL, WHAT HAD she expected, a marriage proposal? She'd only met him five and a half weeks ago, and he wasn't exactly known for being a commitment king. Brooke drove to work, not acknowledging the burning in her eyes, doing her damnedest not to think about the fact that he'd let her walk away.

He'd let her say goodbye.

She pulled into the parking lot. With Zach and Blake both still out, plus several others hit by a flu bug, she was on the B shift for the first time, with a whole new gang, and she found herself working with an EMT named Isobel. Adding to her stress, Brooke was the scheduled driver for the day, which began the moment she got out of her car and the bell rang.

"Watch your speed," was Isobel's most common refrain, uttered every two seconds on every one of their many, *many* calls. Isobel had a cap of dark hair and darker eyes, both her expression and demeanor screaming, *I know I'm a woman in a man's world, but hear me roar.* "Watch that turn—"

"I'm watching."

"Watch—"

"I'll keep watching," Brooke said evenly, each and every time, though by the afternoon, she didn't feel so even. She missed Dustin. "Believe it or not, I've actually driven once or twice before."

"You can never be too careful is all." Isobel eyed the speedometer. "Watch—"

"Okay." Brooke took a deep breath. "Still watching."

"Sorry." Isobel flashed a small, conciliatory smile. "I know I'm a pain. I'm just overly cautious."

Nothing wrong with that. If only Brooke had watched over her own broken heart as cautiously…

Isobel was blessedly quiet until they turned on Third Street, heading toward their call, an outdoor beach café with a kitchen fire, where one of the cooks had passed out from the smoke and hit his head. A hundred yards ahead, the light turned red.

Isobel pointed. "Watch—" Then she caught herself, and cleared her throat. "Nothing."

Brooke pulled up behind two fire trucks. They had the fire contained, but the flames were still impressive, leaping fifty feet into the sky. She and Isobel got out of their rig and immediately one of the firefighters came up to them. "The vic vanished on us. We're still looking for him."

Isobel went back to the radio to report the information. As Brooke took in the fire, she was shocked to see Blake there, standing just off to the side. He was supposed to still be recuperating in the hospital. She'd visited him the day before, and he'd been in no shape to be up. Worried, she moved to his side. "Blake?"

A low, raw sound escaped him and she took a closer look. He wasn't in his gear. He couldn't have been, not with the cast on his leg. His jeans were cut over the cast, and he wore a sweatshirt that looked odd, given it was at least eighty-five degrees outside. He leaned his weight on a crutch, but what caused Brooke concern was how pale he looked, and the fact that he was sweating profusely. "Blake?"

He didn't respond. Eyes locked on the flames, face tight, he seemed miles away.

When she set her hand on his arm, he nearly leaped out of his skin. "Hey, just me." She sent him a smile he didn't return. "You all right?"

"Yes."

"You don't look it. You're in pain."

"Nah. I've got enough pain meds in me to change my name to Anna Nicole Smith."

With a low laugh, she turned back to the rig and saw Isobel had located their vic. He was shaking his head, pushing her hands away before walking off. He didn't seem to want treatment. "Looks like we don't have a transport after all. Can we give you a ride?"

When Blake didn't answer, she looked at him—he was limping away with shocking speed. Running after him, Brooke caught up just as he got as close as he could to the flames without igniting. "Blake, what are you doing?"

At the sound of her voice, he jerked. "Brooke?" He blinked, as if surprised to see her, as if he didn't remember seeing her only two seconds ago.

"Okay, you know what? You're not okay." She put her hand on his arm. "Let's go sit down."

"What are you doing here?"

"I'm working. On you. Why are you out of the hospital?"

"I don't know." He closed his eyes. "I'm sorry. I just...I'm sorry. For everything."

"Come on. Let's get you back." Away from the fire and the pain she suspected he was suffering. "We're in the way here."

He looked around and blanched. "God, I'm sorry."

"For what, Blake?"

"I can't..." He shoved his fingers through his hair and turned away from her, but not before she saw a suspicious sheen to his eyes. "I'm so damned sorry. I should have handled this better. I should have stopped it sooner."

"Blake? Stopped what sooner?"

Staring at the flames, he appeared transfixed. "I don't want to lose another partner. Or a friend."

"What do you mean? Blake, done *what* sooner?"

"Lots of things, actually." He walked off, but again she stopped him.

"I don't think being alone is what you need, Blake."

"Please." He jerked free, his face tortured. "Just leave me alone. There's nothing you can do to stop it from happening."

"What do you mean?" But she was afraid she knew, or at least was starting to know. "Blake—"

"It's not what you think."

But she was suddenly sure it was *exactly* what she thought. The arsonist was someone from within their own ranks. Possibly, terrifyingly, the someone standing right here in front of her. "Okay, let's go over to the ambulance, and—"

"Isobel needs you."

Brooke turned back to the rig and saw Isobel waving at her frantically.

"We have a call!" she was yelling.

Brooke turned back to Blake. "I have to go but I want you to come with me—"

But she was talking to herself. *"Blake?"*

He'd vanished.

17

BROOKE RAN BACK to the rig. Hopping into the driver's seat, she pulled out her cell phone.

"No talking on the phone while you're driving," Isobel said.

"I'm not driving yet." She punched in Zach's cell phone number.

"We have a call. Eighth and Beach."

"I know, but this is an emergency, too." She got Zach's voice mail. Damn it. "Zach," she said, very aware of Isobel listening to every word. "I need to talk to you. ASAP." She shut the phone and tried to order her racing thoughts. "We need to get someone else to take this call. Blake—"

"There is no one else. We need to go, now."

"Fine." She handed her cell over to Isobel. "Call the station, have someone come to get Blake. Then call Tommy Ramirez. Tell him—" What? What the hell could she say? All she had were suspicions. "Tell him I need to talk to him. That it's urgent. Ask him to meet us at the hospital after we pick up our vic."

But Tommy didn't meet her. So after Brooke and Isobel had turned their patient over to the E.R., she tried the chief, and shock of all shocks, got him.

"This better be important, O'Brien," he said in his sharply authoritative voice. "I'm in a meeting."

"It's about Blake."

The chief was silent for a single, long beat. "What about him?"

Brooke moved away from Isobel so that she could speak frankly. "He was at the scene of the Third Street fire today, and he didn't look right. And…" Oh, God, how to say this? "And I think he was trying to confess to arson."

"You *think?* What the hell does that mean? And what arson?"

"He wasn't coherent. He—" She frowned at the static in her ear. "Sir? Hello, Chief?" She'd lost him. *"Shit."*

"You're not supposed to swear while in uniform," Isobel said.

Brooke contained the urge to wrap her fingers around Isobel's neck and drove them back to the station.

The chief was there, waiting for her. "Blake isn't at the hospital or at the fire."

"What's going on?" Cristina stood in the doorway, looking unnerved. "What's the matter with Blake? Eddie went to go get him but he couldn't find him."

"He's missing," the chief said. "And he's not answering his cell."

"He was at the Third Street fire," Brooke told Cristina. "He was walking with a crutch, definitely disoriented— *oh my God.*"

The chief turned on her. "What?"

"What if he went *into* the fire?"

"Why would he do that?" Panic raised Cristina's voice. "He wasn't suited up, he wasn't working—"

"But he wasn't himself," Brooke said slowly, reviewing their conversation. "He was rambling, not making much sense, and just staring at the flames."

"Rambling about what?" Cristina cried.

"He kept saying sorry about the fires, like he was trying to confess."

Cristina gasped and covered her mouth. "He didn't— he wouldn't—"

"He didn't look good, and then we got a call. He'd vanished."

The chief headed for his truck with long strides while Cristina dragged Brooke inside, where she sank to the couch in the living room.

"That building is gone," Brooke said. "Completely gone. I should have stopped him. I should have—"

"You couldn't have stopped him," Sam said, coming in behind them. "And he's not that stupid."

Cristina let out a low sound of grief.

"Look, he hasn't been the same since Lynn died," Sam told her. "We've all tried to talk to him about it, but you know how he is. He's Eeyore. He's stubborn. But not stupid," he repeated. "No way did he go into that fire."

"He was hurting," Cristina whispered. "He lost his partner."

"And *he's* dealing with it." Dustin said this very gently, coming in from the kitchen. "You can't do it for him."

Covering her face, she sank to the couch next to Brooke. "This. *This* is why I like to alienate people. Goddamn it, you made me forget to alienate him and now I care!"

"Cristina." When she didn't answer, Dustin crouched at her side. *"Cristina."*

"Caring sucks," she whispered through her fingers.

He pulled them from her face. "Not always."

She just stared at him.

"Not always," he repeated softly. "What I feel for you doesn't suck. And what I'm hoping you feel for me doesn't suck."

"Damn it." She closed her eyes. "It doesn't. It only scares the living hell out of me. You should brace yourself now." She opened her eyes. "Because I'm maybe falling in love, too. And it's all your fault."

Dustin looked staggered as he drew a shaky breath.

"Don't you have anything to say?"

"Thank you?"

She stared at him, then with a shocked laugh at having her own words tossed back at her, she lunged up and hugged him tight.

Desperate to take her mind off Blake, Brooke tried to be happy for her partner. Putting himself out there had paid off for Dustin, in a big way. It was right then that she realized she hadn't put herself out there for Zach at all. Instead, she'd done the opposite, hiding behind her six-week time limit. She'd even said goodbye already.

"You okay?"

She opened her eyes to Aidan. Was she okay? She was leaving a job she loved in less than a week. Her grandmother's house was all but sold in spite of the fact that beneath all the clutter, she'd discovered a gorgeous, well-tended home that seemed to say *Don't sell me* every time she walked in the door.

The truth was, this decision to move yet again wasn't being dictated by family or school or anything but her own fear.

Funny, really.

And damned ironic.

All her life she'd been racing from one spot to another, and now she was free to do as she chose, go anywhere she wanted, and…and all she wanted was to stay.

With Zach.

"Brooke?"

She looked at Aidan. "It's nothing. I'm fine."

"Even if that was true, if you're fine, how's Zach?"

"When I left there, he was in a little pain but—"

"Not what I meant."

"Yeah." She sighed. "He was…good."

"He's the master at good. Look, I love the guy, but—"

"I'm sure you two will be very happy together."

"You're funny." He shook his head. "Look, neither Zach nor I have ever really needed a woman in our life."

"I know. I get it."

"No, see that's the thing. Zach looks at you differently. He has from the beginning. If you leave, it'll be like losing his parents all over again. Or his brother."

"He lost his brother?"

"Caleb moved to L.A. the day Zach turned eighteen, pretty much deserting him. Can't blame the guy. He hadn't signed on to be a parent, but still, it was rough on Zach. He's not good with opening up. He's afraid."

She tried to picture the big, laid-back, easygoing Zach Thomas afraid of anything. After all, the man faced danger every single day on the job without so much as a flinch.

But that wasn't the same.

In a way, work was much easier because it was pure testosterone and adrenaline. Putting himself on the line probably made Zach feel better about his losses, almost as if he were offering himself up to fate, as well. And as a bonus, he never had to open up emotionally, except with these guys, the brothers of his heart.

She got that; she'd done the same with her chosen career.

But Cristina and Dustin had managed to find something real, and Brooke wanted that. It was time, *past* time, to get it for herself, because if she'd learned anything today, it was that life was too damn short not to go for it. She stood up.

"What are you going to do?"

"It's…complicated."

"The best things are." Aidan hugged her. "I hope it's good complicated."

"I hope so, too."

"I TRIED CALLING you, Zachie."

Zach sat at the side of Phyllis's hospital bed. "I'm sorry. I can't find my cell phone. I think I lost it in the warehouse fire."

"Don't worry." Her voice sounded shaky. "You asked me not to demolish the house if someone asks, and I won't. I was just telling Blake the same thing."

"Blake came here to see you?"

"Yes. He wanted to talk about my house fire."

"Why?"

Phyllis had a razor-sharp memory, but she'd been too doped up on meds for anyone to take advantage of that. Until now, apparently. "Because he was there. Yes," she said at his surprise. "It finally came to me. It was Blake I saw standing on the perimeter of my property, holding a blowtorch."

The air deflated from Zach's lungs. Blake at the scene

just before the fire, with an ignition device… "Phyllis, are you sure?"

"Well, when I brought it up, he said no, my memory was all twisted from the trauma, but…" She shook her head. "But I don't believe it. I remember."

Blake was the missing link? Blake connected all the fires?

Blake was the arsonist?

It made no sense, and yet…and yet in a crazy way it made *perfect* sense—Blake's ongoing obsession with fire, any fire, and his need to be near it, even the bonfire from the chief's birthday party. "Phyllis, listen to me. I need you to trust me, okay? I have to go but I'll be back."

"Will you bring Cecile?"

"I'll bring you more pictures of her, I promise."

When he got to the parking lot and into his truck, he remembered—no cell phone. Running back inside the hospital, he went straight to a pay phone and called Tommy.

Tommy listened to every word and then said, "Go home. You hear me? Get home and keep your ass right there or I'll get it fired."

"You can't do that."

"Trust me, I'll find a way."

Frustration beat at Zach as he drove home, feeling useless and helpless—two emotions he couldn't resent more. God, Blake… *Could it be true?*

And yet the evidence was there, at least circumstantially. The blowtorch at Phyllis's was huge. And he'd been quiet and withdrawn and secretive for months, pushing all of them from his life.

Zach had to go see him, had to look into Blake's eyes and judge for himself.

But Blake wasn't home, so Zach went back to his place and paced a groove into his living room floor, which did nothing for his adrenaline level.

At the knock on his door, he opened it to the one person he'd have given everything to see.

Brooke, still wearing her uniform, eyes shadowed, mouth grim, looking like the best thing he'd seen all damn day.

"Damn, are you a sight for sore eyes," he said.

"I'm not supposed to be here," she said. "I forgot to clock out at work."

"Good. Because I'm not here, either. I'm on my way to find Blake's ass and probably get mine fired."

"You know where he is?"

"No."

They both stood there and stared at each other, unsure what to say next.

"I'm really not here," she finally said again, "telling you that I take back my goodbye."

"Then I'm not really doing this." Hauling her to him, he covered her mouth with his.

She sighed in pleasure and sagged against him, fisting her hands in his shirt to keep him close.

As if that was necessary.

"Zach," she murmured. "We need to talk."

"Yeah."

But then she nipped at his lower lip, making him groan. He stroked his tongue to hers, his hands running down her body, filling them with her glorious curves. "We'll talk," he promised her. "In a minute. Maybe ten." He needed to lose himself in her before he faced the unthinkable—that one of their own was an arsonist.

Not going there, not yet. He kicked the door shut, tugging her upstairs to his bedroom.

She stared at his bed. "First I really need to tell you what I came for—"

"You haven't come yet." He nudged her onto the bed and followed her down. "But you're going to."

18

ZACH'S WORDS sent a shiver of desire skittering down Brooke's spine. In his eyes was a fierce intensity—for her, which she loved, but also the same grief she'd seen in Cristina's.

He knew about Blake.

He kissed her, hard. She knew he was hurting and destroyed over Blake's betrayal, that he was trying to lose himself in her. She understood. She wanted to get lost in him, too.

He pulled off her shirt, and she did the same for his, sliding her hands up his heated skin, feeling the hard planes beneath quiver for more. "Are we letting loose again?"

"No." His mouth slid over her neck, her shoulder, making its way toward a breast. "This time it's more, damn it." He curled his tongue around her nipple.

Sinking her fingers into his hair, she arched up into his mouth. "More?"

"Everything's all fucked up." His voice was low, raw, as he slid a hand into her panties.

His physical pain matched the mental anguish in his eyes, and both broke her heart. "I know."

"Except this, with you." He tugged her panties down to her thighs to give him better access. "I don't usually do this."

"Pull a woman's pants down?"

"No, smart-ass. Get into a relationship."

When his gaze caught hers, she couldn't look away. "Is that what we're doing?"

"I thought you were safe. You're leaving, for Christ's sake. You're outta here. Can't get much safer than that."

Moved by his pain and frustration, she pressed her forehead to his. "Zach."

"I mean, I wasn't going to fall for a woman with one foot already out the door. It was never going to happen."

She closed her eyes.

"But goddamn it, it did."

Before she could open her mouth, he covered it with his. Reality had no place then, no place at all. Until she smelled smoke. "Zach—"

"I know. We're both idiots."

"No." She coughed. *"Smoke."*

"Uh-huh. I think I'm on fire."

"No, I mean *real* smoke." Just as she said this, his smoke alarm went off.

"What the—" Eyes hot, body hard, his face was a mask of frustration as he lifted his head and sniffed the air. "Shit, it *is* smoke." He pulled free and leaped off the bed, staring at the wisps curling beneath the bedroom door.

"Zach!"

"I see it." He tossed her his phone from the night-stand. "Call it in!" He ran into the bathroom, coming out with towels, which he shoved under the door to block the smoke while she called 911.

Coughing, choking, Brooke dashed to the window and then gasped. Zach peered over her shoulder and swore.

Down on the grass far below stood Blake. He was

propped up on one crutch, face gray, holding a blowtorch as he looked right at them.

Zach threw Brooke her clothes and shoved his feet into his jeans. Then he reached under his bed and pulled out a portable rope ladder. "My house is on fire. My damn house is on fire. I'm going to kill him."

But Brooke was still staring at Blake, who had tears running down his face as he limped toward the door, vanishing inside.

"He's in—" Brooke gasped, still coughing. "Zach, Blake's inside." The smoke tightened in her lungs so that she couldn't talk.

Zach covered her mouth with a towel. "Breathe into that." He tossed the ladder out the window. Straddling the ledge, he reached for her. "Come on. You're going down and out. Quickly." He pulled her out the window and onto the rope. "Don't stop until your feet touch the ground. Got that?"

Right. Don't stop. Except she wanted to stop. She wanted to stop time and go back to a few minutes ago, when he'd been about to bury himself deep inside her, telling her he'd fallen. "I'm not leaving you."

"Go!" His voice was already hoarse, his eyes flashing fear and anger. "I'm getting Blake, then I'll be right behind you—"

"Zach—"

"Brooke, listen to me." He gave her a little shake. "You have to be out of here for me to do this."

"But—"

"No, I mean it. I can't lose you. I can't." He set his forehead to hers. "I can't do this with you still in here, in danger."

He meant he couldn't lose another person who meant so much to him. Brooke's heart swelled until it felt too big for her body.

"Please go," he said, hugging her hard. "Because if something happens to you—"

"It won't, it won't. I'm going." She squeezed him tight, breathing through the towel and still coughing. "But you should know something. I love you, Zach."

He looked staggered. "Brooke."

"I do. I love you." It'd probably sound better if she could talk more clearly, but she could tell he understood. "And I swear to God if you die in here, I'll come find you and kill you again."

He choked out a laugh. Off in the distance they could finally hear sirens. *"Go."*

"Going." And down the ladder she went, leaving him to face Blake alone.

Brooke sat on the curb, staring up at the flames. Dustin kept trying to put the oxygen mask over her face, while dabbing at a nasty cut on her arm that she'd managed to get from the rain gutter on her way down the ladder. She kept slapping the mask away, not taking her eyes off the house.

Where was he? Sam, Eddie and Aidan had all gone in after Zach and Blake. Why weren't they—

Finally the door burst open and Sam and Aidan appeared, with Zach between them, Eddie just behind.

No Blake.

Shoving the blanket off her shoulders, Brooke went running toward them.

"Brooke," Zach was saying to Isobel. "Where the hell's Brooke?"

"Here," she managed.

At the sound of her voice he whipped around. He still wore only his Levi's. Dirt and ash were smeared over his chest and torso, blackening the bandages from the last fire he'd been in. He was bleeding from several cuts, as well, and couldn't stop coughing. His eyes were wild, though they calmed at the sight of her as he hauled her into his arms.

"Blake?" she whispered.

Eyes revealing his misery, he shook his head. "We found the blowtorch, and his hard hat. Nothing else."

Heart heavy, she hugged him tight, but she didn't get to hold on to him for long. The scene was chaotic as all hell. Tommy appeared, and the chief, not to mention every rig out of their firehouse, plus too many police units to count.

Zach was pulled aside. "For questioning," Aidan told her.

"He didn't do anything wrong—"

"They know that," he quickly assured her. "But with Blake gone—"

"Gone?"

"They didn't find a body, but—" His voice broke, and he cleared his throat. "But they expect to. There's going to be an internal investigation. Zach wants me to take you to the hospital for stitches—"

"I've got her, you stay with Zach." Dustin flanked her on one side, and Cristina was on the other, looking devastated over the news about her partner.

They took her to the hospital, where she received eight stitches and a tetanus shot. Exhausted and woozy, she let Dustin take her home, where she had a message waiting from her Realtor about the offer on the house.

Was she taking it?

Good question. She'd gotten her asking price. Didn't that just put a nice neat bow on her life. The end of yet another era...

Dustin called in for an update. The fire was out; Blake was presumed dead. Cristina showed up with Thai takeout and a brown bag. The three of them sat around Brooke's table, grimy and filthy, stuffing their faces.

"I still can't believe it was Blake," Cristina said very quietly. "That he—" She broke off, her voice choked. "He was a pyromaniac. In some ways we all are, or we wouldn't do this, but he was mentally ill. Tommy said that looking back, you could see he started unraveling when the chief came from Chicago, right about the time that Lynn died." She closed her eyes. "He needed help."

Dustin squeezed her hand. They ate in silence, an emotional but companionable sort of silence until Cristina looked at the stack of boxes filled with the stuff Brooke hadn't been able to make herself get rid of—the photos, the diaries—all things that had helped Brooke find the missing parts of herself. "Looks like you've been busy, Brooke."

She raised a brow. "Did you just call me Brooke?"

"That is your name, right?"

"I thought it was New Hire to you."

Cristina shrugged. "You stuck."

Her throat tightened. "Yes, but the job's nearly over."

"You could apply for a permanent position."

She'd never done anything permanent. But this, with the people she now thought of as her friends, felt very permanent. And wasn't that part of what she'd been searching for? "I'm ready for the booze now."

Cristina lifted a brow.

"The brown bag you brought. It's alcohol, right?"

Cristina pulled out a bottle of bubble bath and Dustin laughed.

"What?" Cristina demanded.

"You're so damn cute."

"Oh, shut up." Cristina squirmed, looking uncomfortable. "I'm new at this girl-pal stuff, okay? I thought she might want to just soak, and God, I know, it's stupid."

"No." Brooke hugged her. "It's perfect."

They stayed for ice cream, and two more calls for info, of which they got very little except that Zach was still at the fire site.

After Dustin and Cristina left, Brooke drew herself a bubble bath and lay back, soaking.

Thinking…

A knock at her front door stopped that and her heart. It wasn't Zach, it couldn't be Zach. He was no doubt still with the chief and Tommy. It was probably the real estate agent, whom she'd not yet called back. Wasn't ready to call back, not when she felt as if she'd found all her answers right here in this house—answers about her life, and how she wanted to live it. Which was pretty much the opposite of her grandmother and mother.

Brooke didn't want her memories stuck in boxes in some attic. She wanted to share them with real people. She wanted to create new ones every day.

The knock came again. Wrapping herself in a towel, she went to the door. "Who's there?"

"Me."

Oh, God. She whipped open the door.

Zach stood there in his jeans and someone's firefighter jacket, opened so that she could see he was still as grimy as she'd been only a few moments ago. It didn't matter.

One minute she was holding on to the door and the next moment she was holding on to him.

"Brooke," he murmured, his hand fisting in the towel at her back.

She pulled away to look into his face. "Are you all right?"

"Yeah."

"Your house?"

"Not so much."

"Oh, Zach."

"Aidan's putting me up at his place, but I needed to see you."

"I needed to see you, too. Are you sure you're okay?"

"I am now."

"I feel sick about Blake."

"Yeah." Zach blew out a breath. "They found a stack of wire-mesh trash cans in his garage. The chief is saying he was always a pyromaniac, that this job was just a cover to be near fires, that his illness got too much for him so he started setting fires to put them out. Then I started stirring it all up, which made it worse, and he went crazy." He shook his head. "He was one of us, Brooke. How the hell did this happen to one of us?" He turned in a slow circle. "And there's something else bugging the hell out of me. How did Blake manage to order the properties demolished? He didn't have that kind of pull. It doesn't make sense to me."

She just shook her head and hugged him again, closing her eyes to breathe him in. "You're safe. That's all that matters right now. The rest of the questions will get their answers later."

His eyes cut to the stack of boxes. "You've been busy. Did you take the offer on the house?"

"Not yet."

"Where will you go?"

"I—I'm not quite sure."

"You probably have lots of choices," he said quietly, still looking at the boxes.

"I don't know. I like this coast, a lot."

He turned back to her. "Yeah?"

"Yeah." She swallowed past a lump of emotion the size of a basketball. "There's lots of coastal cities hiring EMTs right now."

"Including Santa Rey."

"I know." Brooke ran her hand over his sooty chest. "I have a tub filled with hot, bubbling water. Interested?"

"As long as you're in it."

"That could be arranged."

They ended up draining the tub so he could shower the grime off him first, then filling it back up. Then they climbed in together, her back to his chest, his legs alongside of hers, his arms surrounding her, cast carefully out of the water. For a long moment he just pressed his jaw to hers. "Rationally, I knew you weren't going to die today," he murmured. "But I've found I'm not always rational when it comes to you."

"Ditto." She was grateful that he couldn't see her face, or the tears that suddenly filled her eyes. *Rational* had gone out the window weeks ago, somewhere around that night on a rock overlooking the ocean.

"Brooke?"

She shook her head and forced herself to laugh. "What does rational have to do with us anyway? We just clicked, that's all."

He ran a finger up her wet arm, leaving a trail of

bubbles and goose bumps. "We could keep clicking. If you weren't leaving."

Craning her neck, she looked into his face.

There was no humor in his gaze, not a single drop. "I realized something that first day with you," he said quietly.

"What, that I was going to be a pain in your ass to dump?"

"That my lifestyle, the one I've reveled in for so long, had finally caught up with me and bit me on the ass. Because for the first time since losing my parents, something was going to matter. You were going to matter, Brooke."

She stared at him. "Is that why you wanted to keep this light?"

"That, and because it was what I thought you wanted."

"You told me I shouldn't fall in love with you. Remember?"

"Yeah, that's because I'm insanely stubborn. I've always thought I was so damn brave. I mean I put myself on the line every single day on the job." He laughed, and it was not in amusement. "But not my heart. Never my heart. And that doesn't make me brave at all. It makes me a coward."

His gaze held hers. "Until I met you. I met you and something happened. The walls crumbled. I put my damn heart on the line for the first time in years, with absolutely no backup, no safety net. And it worked. It felt right," he said sounding staggered. "Hell, it felt amazing." Zach shook his head. "I want to be with you, Brooke."

"For tonight."

"For tonight," he agreed. "And tomorrow night, too."

She looked into his eyes, feeling a little kernel of hope and love, so much love she couldn't draw a breath.

"And the night after that. I want all your nights. I love you, Brooke. But there's something even more shocking."

She managed to breathe. "Are you sure? Because that's…that's pretty shocking."

He finally smiled and, oh baby, was it worth the wait. "Turns out I wasn't out there without a backup at all."

"No?" she whispered.

"No." He cupped her face, stroked his thumbs over her jaw. "You're my backup. You're my safety net. You're all that I need."

"So…"

"So stay. Stay here in Santa Rey with me. Or go. But take me with you."

Now Brooke was the one staggered. "You'd leave here?"

"My home is wherever you are."

Twisting all the way around, she propped herself up on his wet chest. "I don't want to go anywhere."

"You don't?"

"Nope. I know you planned to stay at Aidan's house, but I have this big place all to myself, and I don't really want to leave it, or my job. I think New Hire has a certain ring to it, don't you?"

Laughing softly, Zach pulled her close. "How does New Hire *Thomas* sound?"

Her breath caught. She could hardly speak. "Like everything I ever wanted."

SPECIAL EDITION™

NEW YORK TIMES BESTSELLING AUTHOR

DIANA PALMER

A brand-new Long, Tall Texans novel

HEART OF STONE

Feeling unwanted and unloved, Keely returns
to Jacobsville and to Boone Sinclair, a rancher
troubled by his own past. Boone has always
seemed reserved, but now Keely discovers a
sensuality with him that quickly turns to love. Can
they each see past their own scars to let love in?

*Available September 2008
wherever you buy books.*

Visit Silhouette Books at www.eHarlequin.com   SSE24921

Silhouette

Desire

KATHERINE GARBERA

BABY BUSINESS

Cassidy Franzone wants Donovan Tolley,
one of South Carolina's most prestigious
and eligible bachelors. But when she
becomes pregnant with his heir, she is
furious that Donovan uses her and their
child to take over the family business.
Convincing his pregnant ex-fiancée to marry
him now will take all his negotiating
skills, but the greatest risk he faces is
falling for her for real.

**Available August
wherever books are sold.**

Always Powerful, Passionate and Provocative.

Visit Silhouette Books at www.eHarlequin.com   SD76888

SPECIAL EDITION

A late-night walk on the beach resulted
in Trevor Marlowe's heroic rescue of a
drowning woman. He took the amnesia
victim in and dubbed her Venus, for the
goddess who'd emerged from the sea.
It looked as if she might be his goddess of
love, too…until her former fiancé showed
up on Trevor's doorstep.

Don't miss

THE BRIDE WITH
NO NAME

by *USA TODAY* bestselling author
MARIE FERRARELLA

*Available August
wherever you buy books.*

Visit Silhouette Books at www.eHarlequin.com   SSE24917

HARLEQUIN

More Than Words

"The transformation
is the Cinderella story
over and over again."

—**Ruth Renwick,** real-life heroine

*Ruth Renwick is a Harlequin More Than Words
award winner and the founder of **Inside The Dream.***

Discover your inner heroine!

SUPPORTING CAUSES OF CONCERN TO WOMEN ✠ HARLEQUIN
WWW.HARLEQUINMORETHANWORDS.COM

MTW07RR.i

HARLEQUIN

More Than Words

"Every teenager could use a fairy godmother like Ruth."

—**Sherryl Woods,** author

*Sherryl wrote "Black Tie and Promises," inspired by Ruth Renwick, founder of **Inside The Dream**, a nonprofit organization that helps students with economic difficulties attend their high school graduation celebrations.*

Look for *"Black Tie and Promises"* in
More Than Words, Vol. 4,
available in April 2008 at eHarlequin.com
or wherever books are sold.

SUPPORTING CAUSES OF CONCERN TO WOMEN ✠ HARLEQUIN
WWW.HARLEQUINMORETHANWORDS.COM

MTW07RR2

REQUEST YOUR FREE BOOKS!

2 FREE NOVELS PLUS 2 FREE GIFTS!

HARLEQUIN®

Blaze™

Red-hot reads!

YES! Please send me 2 FREE Harlequin® Blaze™ novels and my 2 FREE gifts (gifts are worth about $10). After receiving them, if I don't wish to receive any more books, I can return the shipping statement marked "cancel". If I don't cancel, I will receive 6 brand-new novels every month and be billed just $4.24 per book in the U.S. or $4.71 per book in Canada, plus 25¢ shipping and handling per book and applicable taxes, if any*. That's a savings of 15% or more off the cover price! I understand that accepting the 2 free books and gifts places me under no obligation to buy anything. I can always return a shipment and cancel at any time. Even if I never buy another book, the two free books and gifts are mine to keep forever.

151 HDN ERVA 351 HDN ERUX

Name	(PLEASE PRINT)
Address	Apt. #
City	State/Prov.	Zip/Postal Code

Signature (if under 18, a parent or guardian must sign)

Mail to the Harlequin Reader Service:
IN U.S.A.: P.O. Box 1867, Buffalo, NY 14240-1867
IN CANADA: P.O. Box 609, Fort Erie, Ontario L2A 5X3

Not valid to current subscribers of Harlequin Blaze books.

Want to try two free books from another line?
Call 1-800-873-8635 or visit www.morefreebooks.com.

* Terms and prices subject to change without notice. N.Y. residents add applicable sales tax. Canadian residents will be charged applicable provincial taxes and GST. Offer not valid in Quebec. This offer is limited to one order per household. All orders subject to approval. Credit or debit balances in a customer's account(s) may be offset by any other outstanding balance owed by or to the customer. Please allow 4 to 6 weeks for delivery. Offer available while quantities last.

Your Privacy: Harlequin Books is committed to protecting your privacy. Our Privacy Policy is available online at www.eHarlequin.com or upon request from the Reader Service. From time to time we make our lists of customers available to reputable third parties who may have a product or service of interest to you. If you would prefer we not share your name and address, please check here. ☐

HB08R

HQN™

We *are* romance™

How can he keep his eye on the ball when she's in view?

From *New York Times* bestselling author

carly phillips

Available in July!

Just one short season ago, major-league center fielder
John Roper had it all. But this hot property's lucky streak has
run out. Now it's up to him, and Hot Zone publicist Amy Stone,
to get his life back on track. Amy finds it's easier said than done.
With a crazed fan playing stalker and Roper's refusal to put
his own needs first, she's starting to think that life in the fast
lane isn't all it's cracked up to be. But when the two retreat
to a secluded lodge, the sexy center fielder throws Amy a
curveball—one she never saw coming....

Hot Property

www.HQNBooks.com

PHCP333

HARLEQUIN®

Blaze™

COMING NEXT MONTH

#411 SECRET SEDUCTION Lori Wilde
Perfect Anatomy, Bk. 2

Security specialist Tanner Doyle is an undercover bodyguard protecting surgeon Vanessa Rodriguez at the posh Confidential Rejuvenations clinic. Luckily, keeping the good doctor close to his side won't be a problem—the sizzling sexual chemistry between them is like a fever neither can escape....

#412 THE HELL-RAISER Rhonda Nelson
Men Out of Uniform, Bk. 5

After months of wrangling with her greedy stepmother over her inheritance, the last thing Sarah Jane Walker needs is P.I. Mick Chivers reporting on her every move. Although with sexy Mick around, she's tempted to give him something worth watching....

#413 LIE WITH ME Cara Summers
Lust in Translation

Philly Angelis has been in love with Roman Oliver forever, but he's always treated her like a kid. But not for long... Philly's embarking on a trip to Greece—to find her inner Aphrodite! And heaven help Roman when he catches up with her....

#414 PLEASURE TO THE MAX! Cami Dalton

Cassie Parker gave up believing in fairy tales years ago. So when her aunt sends her a gift—a lover's box, reputed to be able to make fantasies come true—Cassie's not impressed...until a sexy stranger shows up and seduces her on the spot. Now she's starring in an X-rated fairy tale of her very own.

#415 WHISPERS IN THE DARK Kira Sinclair

Radio talk show host Christopher Faulkner, aka Dr. Desire, has been helping people with their sexual hang-ups for years. But when he gets an over-the-air call from vulnerable Karyn Mitchell, he suspects he'll soon be the one in over his head....

#416 FLASHBACK Jill Shalvis
American Heroes: The Firefighters, Bk. 2

Firefighter Aidan Donnelly has always battled flames with trademark icy calm. That is, until a blazing old flame returns—in the shape of sizzling soap star Mackenzie Stafford! Aidan wants to pour water over the unquenchable heat between them. But that just creates more steam....

www.eHarlequin.com

HBCNM0708